A MAGICIAN WONDROUS STRANGE

Peri grunted and shoved her scrub-bucket farther down the hall. The waves of suds she sent across the floor turned into tide and foam.

There was a sudden crash. The inn door, with some-one clinging to it, had blown open under a vigorous puff of spring wind. Peri looked up to see a stranger lose his balance on her tide. He danced upright a moment. Then he tossed his arms, fell, and slid down the hall to kick over her bucket before he washed to a halt under her astonished nose.

They stared at each other, nose to nose. The stranger lay prone, panting slightly. Peri, wordless, sat back on her knees, her brush suspended, dripping on the stran-ger's hair.

He popped a soap bubble with one forefinger and said, "I heard a rumor that someone here needs a magician." He got slowly to his feet and ran a hand down his drip-ping clothes. The dripping stopped. The flagstones were suddenly dry. So was the puddle outside the door.

By Patricia A. McKillip
Published by Ballantine Books:

THE QUEST OF THE RIDDLE-MASTER

THE RIDDLE-MASTER OF HED
HEIR OF SEA AND FIRE
HARPIST IN THE WIND

THE CHANGELING SEA

THE
CHANGELING
SEA

Patricia A. McKillip

A Del Rey Book
BALLANTINE BOOKS • NEW YORK

FOR
JEAN KARL

One

No one really knew where Peri lived the year after the sea took her father and cast his boat, shrouded in a tangle of fishing net, like an empty shell back onto the beach. She came home when she chose to, sat at her mother's hearth without talking, brooding sullenly at the small, quiet house with the glass floats her father had found, colored bubbles of light, still lying on the dusty windowsill, and the same crazy quilt he had slept under still on the bed, and the door open on quiet evenings to the same view of the village and the harbor with the fishing boats homing in on the incoming tide. Sometimes her mother would rouse herself and cook; sometimes Peri would eat, sometimes she wouldn't. She hated the vague, lost expression on her mother's face, her weary movements. Her hair had begun to gray; she never smiled, she never sang. The sea, it seemed to Peri, had taken her mother as well as her father, and left some stranger wandering despairingly among her cooking pots.

Peri was fifteen that year. She worked at the inn beside the harbor, tending fires, scrubbing floors, cleaning rooms, and running up and down the kitchen stairs with meals for the guests. The village was small, poor, one of the many fishing villages tucked into the rocky folds of the island. The island itself was the largest of seven scattered across the blustery northern sea, ruled for four hundred years by the same family.

The king's rich, airy summer house stood on a high crest of land overlooking the village harbor. During the months when he was in residence, the wealthy people of the island came to stay at the inn, to conduct their business at the king's summer court, or sometimes just to catch a glimpse of him riding with his dark-haired son down the long, glistening beaches. In winter, the inn grew quiet; fishers came in the evening to tell fish stories over their beers before they went home to bed. But even then, the innkeeper, a burly, good-natured man, grew testy if he spotted a cobweb in a high corner or a sandy footprint on his flagstones. He kept his inn scoured and full of good smells.

He kept a weather eye on Peri, too, for she had a neglected look about her. She had grown tall without realizing it; her clothes were too loose in some places, too tight in others. Her hair, an awkward color somewhere between pale sand and silt, looked on most days, he thought, as if she had stood on her head and used it for a mop. He gave her things from the kitchen, sometimes, at the end of the day to take home with her: a warm loaf of bread, a dozen mussels, a couple of perch. But he never thought to ask her where she took them.

Occasionally her mother, who had simply stopped thinking and spent her days listening to the ebb and flow of the tide, stirred from her listening. She would trail a hand down Peri's tangled, dirty hair and murmur, "You come and go like a wild thing, child. Sometimes you're there when I look up, sometimes you're not. . . ." Peri would sit mute as a clam, and her mother's attention would stray again to the ceaseless calling of the sea.

Her mother was enchanted, Peri decided. Enchanted by the sea.

She knew the word because the old woman whose house she stayed in had told her tales of marvels and magic, and had taught her what to do with mirrors, and bowls of milk, bent willow twigs buried by moonlight, different kinds of knots, sea water sprinkled at the tide line into the path of the wind. The old woman's enchantments never seemed to work; neither did Peri's. But for some odd reason they fascinated Peri, as if by trying a knot in a piece of string she was binding one stray piece of life to another, bridging by magic the confusing distances between things.

The old woman had lived alone, a couple of miles from the village, in a small house built of driftwood. The house sat well back from the tide against a rocky cliff; it was shielded from the hard winter winds by the cliff and the thick green gorse that overflowed the fallow fields and spilled down around its walls. The old woman had made her living weaving. When Peri was younger, she would come to sit at the woman's side and watch the shuttle dart in and out of the loom. The old woman told stories then, strange, wonderful tales of a land beneath the sea where houses were built of pearls, and a constant, powdery shower of gold fell like light through the deep water from the sunken wrecks of mortals' ships. She was very old; her eyes and hair were the fragile silvery color of moonlit sand. One day, not long after Peri's father had died, the old woman disappeared.

She left a piece of work half-finished on her loom, her door open, and all her odd bits of things she called her "spellbindings" lying on the shelves. Peri went to her house evening after evening, waiting for her to return. She never did. The villagers looked for her a little, then stopped looking. "She was old," they said. "She wandered out of her house and forgot her way back."

"Age takes you that way, sometimes," the innkeeper told Peri. "My old granny went out of the house once to take her hoe to be mended. She came back sitting on a cart tail three days later. She never did tell us where she finally got to. But the hoe was mended."

Peri, used to waiting in the empty driftwood house, simply stayed.

She was fidgety and brusque around people then, anyway, and there was nothing in the house to remind her of her parents, both of them lost, in one way or another, to the sea. She could sit on the doorstep and listen to the tide and glower at the waves breaking against the great, jagged pillars of rock that stood like two doorposts just at the deep water. They were the only pieces of stone cliff left from some earlier time; the sea had nibbled and stormed and worn at the land, pushed it back relentlessly. It was not finished, Peri knew; it would wear at this beach, this cliff, until someday the old woman's house would be underwater. Nothing was safe. Sometimes she threw things into the sea

4

that she had concocted from the old woman's spellbindings: things that might, she vaguely hoped, disturb its relentless workings.

"If you hate the sea so now," Mare asked in wonder one day, "why don't you leave?" Mare was a few years older than Peri, and very pretty. She came to work in the morning, with a private smile in her eyes. Down at the docks, Peri knew, was a young fisherman with the same smile coming and going on his face. Mare was tidy and energetic, unlike Carey, who dreamed that the king's son would come to the inn one day and fall in love with her green eyes and raven tresses. Carey was slow and prone to breaking things. Peri attacked her work grimly, as if she were going to war armed with a dust cloth and a coal scuttle.

"Leave?" she said blankly, knee-deep in suds. Mare was watching her, brows puckered.

"You haven't smiled in months. You barely talk. You scowl out the windows at the waves. You could go inland to the farming villages. Or even to the city. This may be an island, but there are places on it where you'd never hear the sea."

Peri's head twitched, as much away from Mare's reasonable voice as from the sound of the running tide. "No," she said shortly, not knowing why or why not.

Carey giggled. "Can you imagine Peri in the city?" she said. "With her short skirts and her hair like a pile of beached kelp?" Peri glowered at her between two untidy strands of hair.

"No," Mare sighed. "I can't. Peri, you really should—"

"Leave me alone."

"But, girl, you look like—"

5

"I know what I look like," Peri said, though she didn't.

"How will anyone ever fall in love with you looking like that?" Carey asked. Peri's glower turned into such an astonished stare that they both laughed. The innkeeper stuck his head into the room.

"Work on my time," he growled. "Laugh on your own."

They heard him shouting down the kitchen stairs a moment later. "Crab," Carey muttered.

"It's just," Mare said insistently, "you have such pretty eyes, Peri. But nobody can see them with your hair like—"

"I don't want anybody seeing them," Peri said crossly. "Leave me alone."

But later, after she had gone to the driftwood house and made something full of broken bits of glass and crockery and jagged edges of shell to throw into the great sea to give it indigestion, she looked curiously into the old, cracked mirror that the woman had left on her spellbinding shelf. Gray eyes flecked with gold gazed back at her from under a spiky nest of hair. She barely recognized her own face. Her nose was too big, her mouth was pinched. Some stranger was inhabiting her body, too.

"I don't care," she whispered, putting the mirror down. A moment later she picked it up again. Then she put it down, scowling. She went outside to a little cave of gorse where the old woman had found an underground stream wandering toward the sea, and had dug a hole to trap it. Peri knelt at the lip of the well and dunked her head in the water.

Shivering and sputtering, she threw more driftwood on the fire, and sat beside it for an hour, tugging and tugging at her hair with a brush until all the knots came out of it. By that time it was dry, but still she brushed it, tired and half-dreaming, until it rose crackling around her head in a streaky mass of light and dark. She remembered a long time past, when she was small and the old woman had brushed her hair for her, singing . . .

> *"Come out of the sea and into my heart*
> *My dark, my shining love.*
> *Promise we shall never part,*
> *My dark, my singing love. . . ."*

Peri heard her own voice singing in the silence. She stopped abruptly, surprised, and heard then the little, silky sounds of the ebb tide washing against the shore. Her mouth clamped shut. She put the brush down and picked up a clay ball, prickled like a pincushion with bent nails and broken pieces of glass. She flung open the door; firelight ran out ahead of her, down the step onto the sand. But something on the beach kept her lingering in the doorway, puzzled.

There was an odd mass on the tide line. Her eyes, adjusting to moonlight, pieced it together slowly: a horse's head, black against the spangled waves, a long, dark cloak glittering here and there with silver thread, or steel, or pearl. . . . She could not find a face. Then the sea-watcher sensed her watching. A pale, blurred face turned suddenly away from the sea to her, where she stood in the warm light, with her feet bare and her hair streaming away from her face in a wild, fire-edged cloud down her back.

They stared at one another across the dark beach. A

swift, high breaker made the horse shy. The rider swept the cloak back to free his arms; again came a moonlit spark of something rich, unfamiliar. He rode the dark horse out of the sea and Peri closed her door.

"The king came back to the summer house last night," Carey said breathlessly the next morning as the girls put on aprons and collected brooms and buckets in the back room. "I saw his ships in the harbor."

Peri, yawning as the apron strings tangled in her fingers, made a sour noise.

"It's early," Mare commented, surprised. "It's barely spring. The rainy season isn't over yet."

"Prince Kir is with him."

"How do you know?"

"I asked one of the sailors." Carey's eyes shone; she hugged her bucket, seeing visions. "Think of the clothes and the jewels and the horses and the men—"

"Think of the work," Mare sighed, "If they stay from now till summer's end."

"I don't care."

"Jewels?" Peri echoed suddenly. Something teased her brain, a glittering, moonlit darkness. . . .

"Girl, will you wake up?" Mare grabbed Peri's apron strings, tied them impatiently. "This place will be full by nightfall."

There were already strangers in the inn, tracking sand across the floors, demanding fires, spilling things. By the end of the day, the girls were almost too tired to talk. The innkeeper met Peri at the back door and gave her oysters to take home. He studied her, his brows raised.

"You washed your hair!"

It shouldn't have been all that surprising, Peri thought

8

irritably, taking one of the cobbled streets through the village. A moment later she didn't care. She was climbing over a low stone wall to slip burrs into the back pockets of Marl Grey's fishing trousers, hanging on his mother's line. He had called her names a couple of days ago, laughing at her wild hair, her short skirt. "Let's see how funny you look," Peri muttered, "sitting down in a boat on those."

Then she went to see her mother.

She didn't decide to do that; she was just pulled, little by little, on a disjointed path through the village toward her mother's house. She didn't want to go: She hated the still house at the time of day when the boats were coming in. No matter how hard she looked, her father's small blue boat would not be among them. It would be idle, empty, moored to the dock as always. And yet she knew she would look. She opened the gate to her mother's yard. A hoe leaned against the wall among a few troubled clods of dirt. Already the thistles were beginning to sprout.

She went into the house, tumbled the oysters out of her skirt onto the table, and sat down silently beside the fire. Fish chowder simmered in a pot hung over the fire. Her mother sat at the window, gazing at the sunlit harbor. She turned her head vaguely as the shells hit the table, then her attention withdrew. They both sat a few moments without moving, without speaking. Then Peri's mother lifted one hand, let it fall back into her lap with a faint sigh. She got up to stir the soup.

"The king is back," Peri said abruptly, having an uncharacteristic urge to say something. She even, she discovered in surprise, wanted to hear her mother's voice.

"He's early," her mother said disinterestedly.

"Are you making a garden?"

Her mother shrugged the question away. The hoe had been standing up in the weeds for months. Her eyes went to the window; so did Peri's.

The sun was hovering above the horizon, setting the water ablaze. The first of the fishing boats had just entered the harbor; the rest of them were still caught in the lovely, silvery light. Peri's mother drew a soft breath. Her face changed, came gently alive, almost young again, almost the face Peri remembered.

"That's what I dreamed about. . . ."

"What?" Peri said, amazed.

"I dreamed I was watching the sun go down. The way it does just before it dips behind the fog bank, when it burns up the sea and the clouds, and the fishing boats coming home look like they're sailing on light . . . like they're coming from a land you could walk to, if you could step onto the surface of the sea and start walking. It's a country beneath the sea, but in my dream I saw the reflection of it, all pale and fiery in the sunlight. . . . And then the sun went down."

Peri's face was scarlet. "There is no country!" she shouted, and her mother's secret, dreaming face faded away, became the weary stranger's face once more. "There is no magic country in the sea! Stop watching for it!"

But her mother was already watching again. Peri ran out of the house, slamming the door so hard that a flock of sea gulls sunning on the roof wheeled into the air, crying. Her mother's face in the window was still as a sleeper's, hearing nothing in her dreams but the tide.

Two

The next afternoon, Peri climbed the cliff above the old woman's house. There was a moon-shaped patch of sand ringed with gorse at the top; on her days off she could sit in the sunlight and brood at the sea, yet feel protected from the world within the green circle. The gorse was beginning to bloom here and there, tiny golden flowers that made her sneeze. But so far her magic circle was ungilded.

She wrapped her arms around her knees and watched the white gulls wheel above the great weather-beaten spires of rock. Clouds scudded across the sea, making a mysterious weave of light and shadow on the water beyond the spires. Peri frowned at the mystery, chewing a thumbnail. What lay beneath the color and the shadow? Fish? Or some secret world within the kelp that sometimes floated too near the surface of the sea, disturbing those who dwelled on land? What would stop it from troubling her mother? She chewed a fingernail next, then took the finger out of her mouth and drew a spidery design in the sand.

She studied it critically, then drew another one. Hexes, the old woman had called them. She had bent soft willow branches into odd, angular shapes, and then wove webs of thread within them. Hung in doors and windows, they kept malicious goblins and irritating neighbors away. They protected cows from being milked at night by sprites. Perhaps, Peri thought, a few hexes floating across the sea might trap its strange magic underwater. She would make them out of tough dried kelp stalk, row out over the deep water to cast them. She would have to check her father's boat for leaks, get new oars, see if the rudder had been cracked. She had not looked closely at the *Sea Urchin* since the fishers had cleaned the sand and seaweed out of it and moored it in the harbor. Someone had covered it, or it would have sunk under the weight of the heavy winter rains. It probably dragged a crust of barnacles on its bottom. . . .

She drew another hex, a crooked, crabbed design. The wind tossed a gull feather into the circle. She stuck it behind her ear, then broke off a couple of feet of a wild strawberry runner that was gliding across the sand, and wove that absently in and out of her hair. Her dress—her oldest one—barely covered her knees. It was loose around the waist and so tight in the shoulders the seams threatened to part. In the gorse circle, it didn't matter. She stretched out her legs, burrowed her feet under the warm sand, and devised another hex.

I wonder, she thought, if I have to say something over them to make them work. Then she stopped breathing.

A feeling skittered up her backbone. She turned her head slowly, warily, to see who was watching her.

The dark horseman from the sea gazed up at her, mounted at the foot of the cliff. She caught her breath, chilled, as if the sea itself had crept noiselessly across the beach to spill into her circle. Then she blinked, recognizing him. It was only the young prince out for a ride in the bright afternoon. The dark horseman was Kir. Kir was the dark horseman. The phrases turned backward and forward in her mind as she stared at him. A wave boomed and broke behind him, flowing across half the beach, seeking, seeking, then dragged back slowly, powerfully, and, caught in the dark gaze of the rider, his eyes all the twilight colors of the sea, Peri felt as if the undertow had caught her.

Then his face changed again: the king's son, out for a ride. She blushed scarlet.

"Girl," he said, abrupt as one of the rich old lords who came to stay at the inn, though he was not even as old as Mare, "where is the old woman who lives in this house?"

Peri dragged her hair back out of her eyes; the strawberry runner dangled over one ear. "You know her?" she said, surprised.

"Where is she?"

"Gone."

"Where?"

Peri felt a sudden tightness in her throat; her brows pinched together. Too many people gone at once. . . . "She went away and never came back," she said, her sorrow making her cross. "So if you want a spell, you're too late."

"A spell," he repeated curiously. "Was she a witch? Who are you? Her familiar?"

Peri snorted. A waft of pollen from the gorse blooms caught up her nose and she sneezed wildly. The strawberry runner fell over one eye. "I clean rooms at the inn," she said stuffily. "Where do you work?"

He opened his mouth, then paused, his expression unfathomable. His horse shifted restively. There were pearl buttons on his shirt, Peri saw, under his black leather jacket. A ring on his forefinger held a stone that trembled with the same twilight shadows in his eyes. His brows were dark, slightly slanted over his eyes. The bones of his face made hollows and shadows that seemed, in spite of the hearty sunlight, as pale as pearl, as pale as foam.

"I sweep stables," he said at last. "My mother keeps sea horses."

Peri stared at him. A long, dark breaker swept endlessly toward the beach; it curled finally, turning a shade darker just before it crashed against the sand. The prince glanced back at the sound; his eyes, returning to Peri, seemed to carry, for a moment, a reflection of the sea.

"There is no land under the sea," she said uneasily. "There is no land."

His brows closed slightly; his eyes drew at her. "Why do you say that?" he asked abruptly. "Have you seen it?"

"No!" She bored holes in the sand with a twig, scowling at them. She added reluctantly, feeling his attention still pulling at her, "My mother has. In her dreams. So I am laying a hex on the sea."

"A hex!" He sounded too amazed to laugh. "On the entire sea? Why?"

14

"Because the sea stole my father out of his boat and it bewitched my mother so that all she does now is stare out at the water looking for the magic country under the sea."

"The land beneath the sea . . ." A yearning she knew too well had stolen into his eyes, his voice.

"There is no magic country," she said stubbornly, feeling her eyes prick with frustration.

"Then what does she see? And what are you making a hex against?"

Peri was silent. The warm wind bustled into her circle, tossed sand over her hexes, tugged her hair back over her shoulders. The prince's expression changed again, became suddenly peculiar.

"It was you then," he said.

"What was?"

"In the old woman's house, a night ago. You were standing in the doorway with the firelight in your hair, beneath your feet."

"Then it was you," she said, "watching the sea."

"For a moment I thought . . . I don't know what I thought. The light was moving in your hair like tide."

"For a moment I was afraid. I thought you rode out of the sea."

"How could I? There is no kingdom beneath the sea." He watched her a moment longer. Then, silently, he dismounted. He left the black horse flicking its tail at the sand flies, and found the trail through the gorse to the top of the cliff. When he broached Peri's circle, she shifted nervously, for her private sand patch seemed too small to hold such richness, such restlessness. He stood studying her hexes, still silent. Then he knelt in the sand across from her.

"What is your name?"

"Peri."

"What?"

"Peri—Periwinkle."

"Like the sea snail?"

She nodded. "When I was little, my father would spread his nets in the sand to dry, and I would walk on them and pick the periwinkles off."

"My name is Kir."

"I know."

He gave her another of his straight, unfathomable looks. She wondered if he ever smiled. Not, apparently, at barefoot girls who worked at the inn. He traced one of her designs lightly with his finger.

"What is this? Your hex?"

"Yes."

"This will terrify whatever watery kingdom lurks beneath the waves?"

"It's all I can think of," she said grumpily. "I'm trying to remember the old woman's spells. Is that what you wanted from her? A spell?"

"No." He was still gazing at the hex. His face seemed distant, now, aloof; she didn't think he would tell her. But he did, finally. "I wanted to ask her something. I met her one day long ago. I was standing out there watching the sun sinking down between those two stones, and the light on the water making a path from the stones to the sun. She came out to watch me. She said things. Odd things. Stories, maybe. She seemed—she seemed to love the sea. She was so old I thought she must know everything. She—I came here to talk, I wanted to talk. To her."

His eyes had strayed to the sea. His ringed forefinger

moved absently, tracing a private hex in the sand. Peri's eyes moved from the sandy scrawl to the stone on his hand, up to the black pearls on the cuff of his jacket, to the fine cream-colored cloth of his shirt, then, cautiously, to his face. It looked as remote, as expressionless, as the great spires weathering wind and sun and sea. His lashes were black as blackbirds' feathers against his pale skin.

She gave her skirt a sudden tug, trying to pull it over her callused knees. She closed her hands to hide the dry cracks on them. But nothing stayed hidden; she sat there with the king's son in full daylight, with workworn hands and red knees, in an old dress bleached so pale she'd forgotten what color it had ever been. She sighed, then wondered at herself. What did it matter, anyway? What was the matter with her?

The prince heard her sigh under the sigh of the tide; his head turned. He asked curiously, "How will you get these hexes out of the sand and into the sea?"

"I'll make them out of twigs and dry seaweed. I'll bend them and bind the ends, and weave the patterns inside with thread. Then I'll row out in my father's boat over deep water and throw them in."

"Will you—" He stopped, looked suddenly away from her. He began again, his hands closed tightly on his knees. "Will you give the sea a message for me? Will you bind it to one of the hexes?"

She nodded mutely, astonished. "What message?"

"I'll bring it here. When will you lay your hex on the sea?"

"On my next day off. In six days."

"I'll bring it when I can." He glanced at the sun, then over her shoulder at the summer house on its smooth green perch high above the sea. "I must go. I'll leave the message in the house if you're not here."

"I won't be," she said as he rose. "I mean, I'll be working."

He nodded. "But I'll come again," he said, "to see you. To find out what your hex did to the sea." He smiled then, a bittersweet smile that made her stare at him as he picked his way back down the cliff. Mounted, he glanced back at her once, then rode away: the dark horseman, the king's son, who was going to knock on Peri's door like any fisher's son, with a message for the sea.

She found his message on her table four days later among the hexes. The hexes, irregular circles and squares of sticks and seaweed, with jagged spiderwebs of black thread woven across them, carried, Peri thought, a nicely malevolent message. The prince's message was unexpected.

It was a small bundle of things tied up in a handkerchief so soft that its threads snagged on Peri's rough fingers. It was bordered with fine, heavy lace; one corner was embroidered with a pale crown and two letters: QV. Not Kir's initials. Puzzled, Peri untied the ribbon around it.

She sat fingering the small things within, one by one. A short black lock of hair. Kir's? A black pearl that was not round but elongated, irregular, tormented out of shape. Another lock of hair, black, streaked with gray. A ring of pure silver, with initials stamped into it. KUV. Kir? But who was Q? Then she dropped the ring as if it burned, and huddled on her stool as if the king himself had come into her house.

Q,K. Queen, king. King Ustav Var. Kir's father. That was his graying hair lying there on her table.

She tied everything back up, her fingers shaking, averting her eyes, as if she had caught the king in the middle of some small private act—counting the veins in his eyes or contemplating his naked feet to see how the years were aging them. She stuffed the handkerchief into an empty clay jar on the spellbinding shelf and slammed the lid down on it.

There was no way, she had to admit finally, that she could row out to sea in the *Sea Urchin* by herself. Her back and arms were strong from carrying buckets of water and loads of wood, but it took more strength than she possessed to control heavy oars in open water with the sea roiling and frisking under her boat. Just getting out of the harbor with the hard waves feathering into the air above the breakwaters would be a nightmare. She'd lose the oars, she'd have to be rescued, teased and scolded by the fishers. Even the women who fished—Leih and Bel and Ami—were twice her size, with muscles like stones and hands hard as fence slats with rowing calluses.

But how could she get the hexes out so far that the sea would not simply spit them back at her?

She thought about the problem, her brows pinched tight as she worked. Carey was chattering about things she had seen unloaded from the king's ship: carved and gilded chests, milk-white horses, gray dogs as tall as ponies, with lean flanks and slender muzzles, and silver-gray eyes, looking as glazed and panicked as fine ladies from being tossed about on the sea.

"And their collars," Carey breathed, "studded with emeralds."

"Emeralds, my foot," Mare said witheringly. "Glass, girl, glass. This isn't such a wealthy land that the king would waste emeralds on a dog. Peri, your hair is in your bucket."

Peri twitched it out; a tangle landed soddenly on her shoulder. She wiped her nose with the back of her hand, thinking of the pearls on Kir's shirt, the silver ring.

"I want emeralds," Carey said dreamily. "And gowns of white lace and gold rings and—"

"You won't get them on your knees in the soapsuds."

"Yesterday when I brought clean towels to one of the rooms, a man in green velvet said I was beautiful and kissed me."

"Carey!" Mare said, shocked. "You watch yourself. Those fine men will migrate like geese in autumn, and you'll be stuck here with a belly full of trouble."

Carey scrubbed silently, sulking. Peri swam out of her thoughts, glanced up.

"Was it nice?" she asked curiously. For a moment Carey didn't answer. Then her mouth crooked wryly and she shrugged.

"His mustache smelled of beer."

"Green velvet," Mare muttered. "I hope a good wave douses him."

The tide was low that afternoon as Peri walked home, so low that even the great jagged spires stood naked in the glistening sand, and all the starfish and anemones and urchins that clung to their battered flanks were exposed. It was a rare tide. Beyond the spires the sea dreamed gently, a pale milky blue shot with sudden fires from the setting sun. Peri, her shoes slung over

20

her shoulder, watched the bubbles from burrowing clams pop in the wet sand under her feet. The air was warm, silken, promising longer, lazy days, more light, promising all the soft, mysterious smells and colors of spring after the harsh gray winter. The sand itself was streaked with color from the sunset. Peri lifted her eyes, watched the distant sheen of light beneath the sun fall on water so still it seemed she could simply turn toward the tide and follow it. Her steps slowed, her lips parted; her eyes were full of light, spellbound. She could take the path of the sun to the sun, she could walk on the soft opal breast of the ocean as simply as she walked on the earth, until she found, there in the great glittering heart of light, the golden kingdom, the kingdom of—

She stopped, shaking her head free of thoughts like a dog shaking water off itself. Then she began to run.

She flung her shoes in a corner of the house, snatched the hexes from the table, Kir's message from the jar, ran back out, straight across the beach toward the spires and the sun illumining the false, tempting dream between them, as if they were some broken ancient doorway into the country beneath the waves, reflected in the light.

She stood between the spires at the edge of the idle tide, going no farther than that because the sand sloped sharply beyond the spires into deep water. She lifted the hexes, tied together and weighted with Kir's message, threw them with all her strength into the sea.

"I hex you," she shouted, searching for words as bitter as brine to cast back at the sea. "I hate you, I curse you, I lay a hex on you, Sea, so that all your spellbindings will unravel, and all your magic is confused, and so that you never again take anything or anyone who belongs to us, and you let go of whatever you have—''

She stopped, for the hexes, floating lightly along the crest of a wave, had suddenly disappeared. She waited, staring at the water, wanting nothing to happen, wanting something to happen. A bubble popped like a belch on the surface of the water a few yards away. She edged close to the wet starfish-dotted flank of one of the spires. Had she, she wondered uneasily, finally got the sea's attention?

The water beyond the spires heaved upward, flaming red. Peri shrieked. Still it lifted, blocking the sun: a wall of red, streaming waterfalls. Two huge pools of fire hung where the sun had been, so big she could have rowed the *Sea Urchin* into either one of them. Long, long streamers of fire surfaced, eddied gracefully in the tide. And then gold struck her eyes, brighter than the sun.

She gasped, blinking, and the round pools of fire blinked back at her. A sigh, smelling of shrimp and seaweed, wafted over the water.

She edged backward, trying at the same time to cling to the rock like a barnacle. "Oh," she breathed, her throat so full and dry with terror she barely made a sound. "Oh."

In the deep waters beyond the stones, a great flaming sea-thing gazed back at her, big as a house or two, its mouth a strainer like the mouth of a baleen whale, its translucent, fiery streamers coiling and uncoiling languorously in the warm waters. The brow fins over its wide eyes gave it a surprised expression.

Around its neck, like a dog collar, was a massive chain of pure gold.

Three ⁓⊶⥲

Peri stayed with her mother that night. The sea, she decided, annoyed at her constant harassment, had sent some great monster out of its depths to eat her. Her mother didn't ask why she was there, but Peri's presence seemed to tug at her thoughts. She watched Peri. Sometimes a question trembled in her eyes; she seemed about to speak. But Peri would look away. Though seadragons garlanded with gold rode the waves in Peri's mind, she clamped the secret behind her lips, like an oyster locking away its pearl, rather than admit her mother might be right: There might be a land of light and shadow hidden among the slowly swaying kelp beneath the waves.

And Kir. His face rose clearly in her thoughts just before she fell asleep, pale and dark and restless against the vast wild blue of the sea. What message had he sent? she wondered in her dreams. And to whom?

The lovely promises of spring were nothing but

dreams themselves by morning: The spring rains had started. Peri, walking soggily to the inn, felt all her fears of the sea-dragon dwindle under the dreary sky. Nothing alive in the world could have been as big as she remembered it. The gold around its neck could not have been real. And if it had wanted to eat her, it could have plucked her like an anemone away from the rock, the way she'd stood there frozen. Besides, she remembered, cheering up, it had no teeth. Only tiny shrimp and bits of kelp could pass through the strainer in its jaws; it was destined to a life of broth. It had simply been some great sea creature coming up for air as it passed along the island. It was probably scaring ships in the South Isles by now.

But who had put the chain around its neck?

She thought about that as she swept the stairs and made beds and carried buckets of ash to the bins behind the kitchen. Everyone was grumpy because of the rain. The guests tracked paths of water and mud on the floors and complained of smoking chimneys. Some of the fishers came in early off the heavy, swollen sea and trailed in more water, more sand. By the day's end, Peri felt as scoured as the flagstones and as damp. Carey burst into tears.

"My hands," she wailed. "I might as well be an old lobster."

"Never mind," Mare sighed. "Maybe you'll find some rich old lobster to love you."

"I won't! Ever! I'll never get out of this town. I'll never get out of this inn! I'll be scrubbing floors here when I'm ninety years old, and cleaning hearths and making beds to my dying day. The only pearls I'll ever see will be on someone else's fingers, I'll never wear velvet, I'll never sleep in lace, I'll never—"

"Oh, please, Carey. I've got a headache as it is."

"I'll never—"

"You'll never guess—" said Mare's lover, Enin, sticking his head into the doorway of the back room where they hung their aprons and stored their mops. Then he saw Carey's tears and ducked back nervously. "Oh."

"Enin!" Mare called. He was running water, too, from his rain cloak; his boat had just got in. Peri dumped her mop and her brush into her empty bucket and shoved it against the wall. She put her hands to her tailbone and bent backward, stretching. Enin's face reappeared. It was softly bearded, sunburned, and speckled with rain. His eyes, light blue, looked round as coins. Carey banged her brush into her bucket crossly, still sniffing. Enin's eyes went to her cautiously. Mare said, beginning to smile, since Enin's face was the most cheerful thing they had seen all day, "I'll never guess what?"

"You'll never guess what's out there in the sea."

"Mermaids in a coracle, I suppose."

"No." He shook his head, groping for words. "No. It's—"

"A sea monster?"

"Yes!" Peri's mop slipped as she stood staring at him. It rapped her on the head and Enin winced. "Are you all right there, girl? Mare, it's huge! Big as this inn! It came right up to our boats—mine and Tull Olney's—we went farthest out—and watched us fish!"

"Oh, Enin," Mare said, touching his forehead.

"Red as fire, even in the mist and rain, we could see that. And you'll never guess what else."

"It has a chain of gold around its neck," Peri said.

"It's wearing a chain of gold—pure gold—Mare, I swear! Stop laughing and listen!" Then he stopped talking, and Mare stopped laughing, and Carey stopped snuffling. They all stared at Peri.

"I saw it," she said, awkward in the sudden silence. "I saw it. Yesterday. Beyond the spires. The gold hurt my eyes."

Carey's long, slow breath sounded like the outgoing tide. "Gold."

"But what is it?" Mare said, bewildered. "Some great fish? A sea lion with a pattern around its neck?"

"No, no, bigger. Much bigger. More like a—a dragon, yes, that's what it's more like. And the gold is—Ah, Mare, you wouldn't believe—"

"You're right, I wouldn't." Mare sighed. "Probably some poor lost sea-something with a king's gilded anchor chain caught around its neck."

"No."

"No," Peri echoed him. "It's real. I saw the sun pouring off it like—like melting butter."

"Why didn't you tell us?" Carey demanded.

"Because it scared me," she said irritably. "All chained like that. Like someone's pet. I didn't want to think who might have made that chain. The links are so big I could have crawled through one."

There was silence. Carey said suddenly to Enin, "Come in and shut the door."

Her voice was so high and sharp he did it. The noise from the inn faded.

"Why?" he said, puzzled.

"Because it's ours," she said fiercely. "Our gold. It

26

belongs to us, to the village. Not to the king, not to the summer guests. To us. We have to find a way to get it."

Enin stared at her, breathing out of his mouth. Mare pushed her hands against her eyes.

"Oh, Carey."

"She's right, though," Enin said slowly. "She's right."

"It must be our secret," Carey insisted.

"Yes."

Mare turned abruptly, picked her cloak off a peg, and tossed it over her shoulders so fast it billowed like a sail. "I think," she said tautly, "you'd better take another look at this sea-dragon before you start counting your gold pieces. I think—"

"Mare—"

"I think you and Tull had too many beers for breakfast and you rowed right into the place where the sky touches the sea and you hear singing in the mist, and sea cows turn into mermaids, and old ships full of ghosts sail by without a sound. That's where you've been. Sea-dragons. Gold chains." She jerked the door open. "I have a headache and I'm famished. The only gold I want to see is in a cold glass of beer."

"But, Mare," Enin said, following her out. Carey gazed at Peri, her eyes suddenly wistful.

"Was that it? A sea-dream?"

Peri dragged a hand through her hair. "I didn't have any beer for breakfast when I saw it," she sighed. "I don't know what it is. But it's not our gold. I wouldn't like to be caught stealing from whoever made that chain."

Carey was silent; they both were, envisioning gold, so much gold that the damp air seemed to brighten around them. Carey reached for her cloak. "Nonsense," she said briskly. "Anyone who could waste that much gold on a chain for a sea-pet would never know it was missing."

Peri kept an eye out for the sea-pet when she walked back to the old woman's house. But there was no fire in the gray world, no gold, only the sea heaving sullenly between the spires. The rain clouds hiding the setting sun did not release a single thread of light. A false light dragged Peri's eyes from the sea; the gorse blazing gold above the old woman's house. And in front of her house: a black horse.

The rider, apparently, was inside. Peri's brows went up as high as they could go. As she trudged from the tide line across the stretch of beach toward the house, she saw that the top half of the door was open. Kir leaned against the bottom half, watching the breakers so intently that he did not notice Peri until she was nearly on the doorstep.

His head turned, his eyes still full of the sea. His thoughts tumbled over Peri like a wave, drenching her with a sharp, wild sense of restlessness and despair. She stopped short, one foot on the doorstep, staring at him. But he had already moved to open the door, while something shut itself away behind his face.

He didn't speak. Peri dumped scallops the innkeeper had given her out of her cloak and hung it up. He had started a fire, she noticed in surprise. He had picked up driftwood with his royal hands and piled it into the grate. But, it appeared, he did not know what a scallop was.

"What's this?" He was fingering a fan-shaped shell.

"My supper," Peri said, huddling close to the fire. He

watched her shake water out of her hair. She added gruffly, recalling some manners, "You're welcome to stay."

He turned edgily away from the shells. "You cook, too."

"I have to eat," she said simply. He paced to the door and back again to the hearth, where she crouched, combing her hair with her fingers.

"Did you give my message to the sea?" he asked abruptly. She nodded, opening her mouth, but he had turned away again, speaking bitterly before she could answer. "I'm being stupid. It's just a child's game, your hexes, my message. They're probably lying out there now among the litter on the tide line. You can't talk to the sea by throwing things at it."

Peri, trying so hard to understand him that her forehead creased and her eyes were round as owls' eyes, asked bewilderedly, "Why did you want the sea to have your father's ring?"

"Why do you think?" he answered sharply.

"I don't know." She felt stupid herself. Something in her voice made him look at her again, as if he had never really seen her since she walked in damp and untidy from the rain, with red, chapped hands and tired eyes. His expression changed. Peri, recognizing his unhappiness if nothing else, said helplessly, "I don't know if the sea got your message. But after I threw it in, the biggest sea-thing I have ever seen in the world lifted its head out of the water to look at me. Around its neck there was a chain of gold—"

"What?"

"A chain. Gold. It—"

"Are you," he asked, his voice so thin and icy she shifted nearer to the fire, "making a fool of me?"

shook her head, remembering the flame-colored rising out of the sea, blocking the sun, and the molten reflection of gold everywhere. "It was like a dragon. But with fins and long ribbons of streamers instead of wings. It was bigger than this house, and the gold chain ran down into the deep sea as if—as if it began there, at the bottom."

The prince's pale face seemed to glisten in the firelight like mother-of-pearl. He whirled; rain and wind blew across the threshold as he flung open the door. The waves fell in long, weary sighs against the sand. He stood silently, his eyes on the empty sea between the spires. Peri, her clothes still damp, began to shiver.

She moved finally to stop the shivering. She poured water from a bucket into a pot, dropped the scallops into it to steam them open. She hung the pot above the fire, then knelt to add more driftwood to the flames. Kir shut the door finally. He came to the hearth, stood close to Peri. Behind him he had left a trail of wet footprints.

Her eyes were drawn to them; her hands slowed. She heard Kir whisper, "All that gold to keep a sea-thing chained to the bottom of the sea."

"Why—" Her voice caught. "Why would—Who would—"

"There must be a way. There must be." He was still whispering. His hands were clenched. She stared up at him.

"To do what?"

"To get there."

"Where?" She rose, as he flung his wet cloak back over his shoulders. "Where are you going?"

"To the land beneath the sea."

"Now?"

"Not now," he said impatiently. "Now, I'm just going."

"Don't you want supper?"

He shook his head, his attention already ebbing away from her, caught in the evening tide. She scratched her head with a spoon, her face puckered anxiously. "Will you be back?" she asked suddenly. He looked at her from a long distance, farther than sleep, farther, it seemed, than from where the tide began.

"From where?"

She swallowed, feeling her face redden. "Here," she said gruffly. "Will you come back here?"

"Oh," he said, surprisedly. "Of course."

The door closed. She heard his horse nicker, then heard its hoofbeats, riding away from the village, down the long beach into the gathering night. She gazed at the door, envisioning Kir, dark and wet as the night he rode into, restless as the crying gulls and sea winds, with a hint of foam in the color of his skin. A frown crept into her eyes. Her foot tapped on the floor, on one of his footprints. He had left water everywhere, it seemed. Then her foot stilled; her breath stilled. She glimpsed something as elusive as a spangle of moonlight on the water. A lock of his father's hair thrown to the sea, a pearl . . . a message. . . .

She blinked, shaking her head until the odd thoughts and images jumbled senselessly, harmlessly. She grabbed the broom, swept at his watery footsteps across her threshold, at her hearth; they blurred and finally faded.

Four ❧

The rain withdrew, crouched at the horizon; the fishers had a spell of blue sky to tempt them out, and then a wind and a rain-pocked sea to drive them back into the harbor. Out, in, out, in—it was like that for several days. Tales of the sea-dragon became as common as oysters. Then the teasing weather gave way to a full-blown storm that piled surf on the beach and tossed boats loose from the docks. The fishers could not get out past the swells raging at the harbor mouth. The sea-dragon rode out the storm alone. The fishers congregated at the inn to drink beer and stare moodily out at the weather. The guests, disdainful of the smells of wet wool and brine, withdrew to a private room, leaving the hearth and the flowing tap to the villagers. Peri, passing in the hall with her arms full of linen, or coming in to tend the fire, was aware, without really listening, of the thread of gold, glittering and magical, that wove in and out of their conversation.

"Links of gold. A link has to have an opening point, otherwise how would you make a chain? So we'll get a big lever of some kind, force a link apart—"

"And what's the monster going to be doing while you're standing on its neck and sticking a lever through its chain? Nibbling shrimp and watching gulls? It'll dive, man, and take you right down with it."

"Fire, then. Fire melts gold. We'll build a floating forge, row it out underneath the chain where it meets the sea. We'll distract the sea-monster with fish or whatever it eats—"

"Shrimp. Brine shrimp. How can you distract something as big as a barn with something you can hardly see yourself?"

"Then we'll sing to it. It likes singing."

"Sing!"

"Or Tull can play his fiddle. It'll be listening; we'll float the forge behind it, melt a link through, and then . . ."

"Gold," Mare sighed, mopping up the perpetual river of sand and water in the hall. "That's all they talk about these days. Even Ami and Bel. Enin's the worst. It's making them all loony."

"If it's out there," Carey said sharply, "they should get it. It's not doing the monster any good."

"Yes, but they're not thinking. None of them are. Nothing human could make a chain like that. That's what they should be considering first. Instead"—she gave her mop a worried, impatient shove—"they're going to do something stupid. I know it."

"The thing is," the fishers said, while the wind blustered and threatened at the closed windows, "there's still another problem. Even if we do pry open a link, what's the good of that? How could we possibly keep the chain from sliding back down to the bottom of the sea? It'd be like taking a whale into our boats. It'd crush us if we tried to hold it.''

"Then we'll cut a link farther down. We'll kill the monster and let the sea itself float it to shore.''

"Kill it! If we injure it at all, it'll just disappear on us. Or worse, come back and swamp our boats for us.''

"Then how? How do we get the gold?''

Carey took to lingering in the doorway, listening. Peri was tempted to do the same. The fiery sea-dragon with its gold chain provided the only color in a world where everything—sand, sea, sky—had faded gray in the rain. It seemed a wonderful tale for a bleak, idle day, an elaborate fish story to tell over beer beside a warm hearth.

But Mare, bringing clean glasses into the bar, said crossly, "That's like you, all of you, to think of killing when you think of gold.''

Enin said uncomfortably, "Now, Mare, we're just talking, let us be. It's the most we can do on a day like this.''

"But you're not thinking!''

"Well,'' Ami said good-humoredly, "nobody pays us for that.''

"Have you ever met a man or woman who could make a chain like that? Suppose whoever made that chain has something to say about your stealing that gold? Or freeing the sea-monster?''

"Oh, it's probably ancient, Mare, it's probably—''

"Oh, ho, then why is it so shiny it's left its reflection in all your greedy eyes? I haven't heard of so much as a barnacle on it, or a bit of moss. I think you should be a bit careful about who might treat a sea-monster

34

that size like a pet. That's what I think, and there's no need to pay me for it.''

They still talked, for the winds whipped up foam like the froth on cream on the surface of the sea, and the cold rain blew in sheets. But Mare had veered them away from the sea-dragon, Peri noticed. Now it was not "how?" but "who?" and no longer sea-monsters, but enchanted lands and witchery.

"Come to think of it,'' the fishers asked one another, "who did make that chain?''

Lands were invented on distant islands, at the bottom of the sea, or even floating upon the surface of the sea.

"Like the kelp islands, you see. Only they can skim the surface faster than a gull, and fade like light fades on the water, leaving no trace. Beautiful, rich, great floating islands of pearl and coral and gold. . . . The sea people keep the sea-monster the way a child keeps a pet. It's chained to the invisible island.''

"It's not a pet. It's someone who did an evil deed, or crossed a wicked mage, and got chained to the sea bottom in punishment.''

"It wants to be free then.''

"It wants us to break the chain.''

"Suppose we did. Will this wicked mage let us take his gold?''

"Ah, we should get the gold first and worry later.''

Peri, working her mop desultorily, found herself day-dreaming. Distant isles on the top of the world, past the glaciers and icebergs, past the winter lands, beyond winter itself, gleamed like summer light in her head. Magical isles, where fruit was forever ripe and sweet, and the warm air smelled of roses. Lands deep in the sea, where entire cities were made of pearls, and men and women wore garments of fish scales that floated about them in soft, silvery clouds. One of them had fashioned a chain of gold for a very special . . .

"Mare," she said abruptly.

"What?"

"Why do people do things?"

"Why? For as many reasons as there are fish in the sea."

"I mean, if you made a chain for a sea-dragon, would it be because you loved it and didn't want it freed? Or because you hated it and took away its freedom? Or because you were afraid of it?"

"Any one of those things. Why?"

"I was just wondering . . . was it love or hate or fear that made a chain like that?"

Mare looked surprised; Peri rarely used such complicated words. "I don't know. But the way they're talking in there, I think we'll soon find out."

Walking home wearily that afternoon, Peri searched the horizon for one hint of light in the monotonous gray of sea and sky. Rain flicked against her eyes; she pulled the hood of her cloak more closely about her face. Nothing but the slick, mute fish could possibly dwell in that sea, she decided. There were no wondrous deep-sea lands full of castles made of pearl and whalebone. No free-floating islands of perpetual summer. The sea-dragon's chain was nothing more than a ring of kelp that glowed with tiny, gold, phosphorescent sea animals. The sea-dragon itself had probably strayed from warm, distant waters where, in its own sea, it wasn't a monster. That was all. No mystery. Nothing strange, everything explained—

And there it was, beyond the spires, rising up out of

the stormy waters, bright as flame, with the sunlight itself looped around its neck.

It was watching the only movement on the beach: Peri.

She stopped, her mouth open. It lingered, massive and curious, its bright streamers swirling in the restless water. The delicate brow fins over its great eyes flicked up and down like eyebrows. It had a mustache of thin streamers above its mouth. It washed to and fro in the water, its eyes like twin red suns hovering above the sea. It seemed to wash closer with the tide. Peri stepped back nervously and bumped into something that snorted gently between her shoulder blades.

She whirled, gasping. Kir's black mount whuffed at her again. Kir, never taking his eyes from the sea-dragon, held out his hand.

"Come up."

She stepped onto his boot, hoisted herself awkwardly behind him. He said nothing else, just sat there watching the sea-dragon, his eyes narrowed against the rain. It seemed to watch them as intently, all its fins and long streamers roiling to keep its balance in the storm.

And then it was gone, sliding fishlike back into its secret world.

Peri felt Kir draw a soundless breath. Then he lifted the reins, nudged his horse into a sudden gallop, Peri clutched wildly at him. He started under her touch, and slowed quickly.

"I'm sorry—I forgot you were there."

"I'll walk home," Peri suggested breathlessly.

"I'll take you." But he rode slowly in the hard rain, his face turned always toward the sea.

"What is it?" Peri asked again. "Where does the chain begin?"

For a long moment he didn't answer; she began to feel like a barnacle talking to the rock it was attached to. Then he answered her. "I think," he said, so softly she had to strain through the sound of the wind and the waves to hear him, "it begins in my father's heart."

Peri felt herself go brittle, like a dried starfish. Her mouth opened, but no words came out. Then she felt Kir shudder in her arms, and she could move again, the thoughts in her head as vague and elusive as shapes in deep water.

"There is a land under the sea."

"There must be," he whispered.

"That's what you look for, when you watch the sea."

"Yes."

"The way to get there. Where you—where you want to be."

"No one," he whispered. "No one knows this but you."

She swallowed drily, her voice gone again. Unguided, the horse had stopped; rain gusted over them. Kir's face lifted to the touch of water.

"It's why we came here early this year. I am not able, any longer, to be too far from the sea. My father—he thinks—I let him believe that I've lost my heart to some lord's daughter who lives near here. He doesn't suspect that I would give my heart to anyone who would show me the path to that secret country beneath the waves."

"But how—" Peri said huskily.

"Oh, Peri, do I have to spell it out to you? Are you that innocent?"

She thought a moment. Then she nodded, her face

chilled as from inside, from a cold that had nothing to do with the rain. "I must be."

"My father took a lover out of the sea."

"A lover," she whispered.

"Yes."

"The king did." She thought of the lock of his gray hair, falling into the water. "That sounds cold."

"She bore me and gave me to him."

"Then he does know about you."

"No. He doesn't."

"I don't understand," she said numbly.

"I didn't, either, for a long time. . . . Even in the middle of this island, at the farthest point from the sea, I hear the tide, I know when it changes. I dream of the sea, I want to breathe it like air, I want to wear it like skin. But my father said my mother was a lady of the North Isles, with golden hair and a sweet voice, and that she bore me and died. . . . But how could she have had a son who wants to trade places with every fish he sees? I don't know where her son is. But I am not hers. My mother is tide, is pearl, is all the darkness and the shining in the sea. . . ."

A wave roared and broke; a lacework of foam unrolled across the sand almost to the horse's hooves. It withdrew before it touched them; the prince watched it recede. Peri felt herself shivering uncontrollably. Kir made a small sound, remembering her again. He gathered the reins; within minutes Peri was at her door.

She slid down; Kir's eyes were on her face for once, instead of the sea. "I'll come again," he told her, inarguable as tide, and she nodded, speechless but relieved that he was not going to leave her alone with this magical and frightening tale. She looked up at him finally, when he didn't ride away, and saw a sudden, strange relief in his own eyes. He left her then; she watched him until the sea mist swallowed him.

She was so quiet the next day at the inn that Mare said in amazement, "Peri, you look as if you're trying to swallow a thought or choke on it. Are you in love?"

Peri stared at her as if she were speaking a peculiar language. "I'm catching cold," she mumbled, for something to say. "All this rain. I stood in it yesterday watching the sea-dragon."

"You saw it?" Carey's voice squealed. "Why didn't you tell us?"

"I forgot."

"You forgot!" She hugged her wet scrub brush anxiously. "Is it true, then? About the gold? It wasn't a dream?"

"It's real."

"Is it dangerous?" Mare asked worriedly. "Would it attack the boats?"

Peri shook her head, shoving her bucket forward. "It seems friendly."

"Friendly!"

"Well, it seems to like watching people."

"That's what Enin said, that it likes listening to the fishers talk. He says it pokes its big head out of the water and listens, while the gulls land on it and pick at the little fish caught in its streamers."

"I bet it wouldn't miss that chain," Carey murmured.

"Yes, but how could they possibly get it off?" Mare said. "It sounds enormous. Whoever put it on meant it to stay."

"But they have to get it off!" Carey protested. "They have to! We'll all be rich! If it was put on, then it can be taken off."

Peri ducked over her work, thinking of Kir watching the cold, tantalizing waves, of the great chain disappearing down, down into a secret place. "Magic," she said, and was surprised at the sound of her voice.

Carey stared at her, openmouthed. "What's magic?"

"The chain. It must be."

"You mean wizards and spells, things like that?"

Mare straightened slowly, blinking at Peri. "You're right. You must be." A door slammed within the inn; she picked up the hearth brush again. "If magic put it on, then magic must take it off."

"It's not magic," the innkeeper said testily, poking his head into the room, "that does your work for you, as much as you may wish it." All their brooms and dust cloths moved again, to the beat of his footsteps down the hall. The front door opened; a wet wind gusted across the threshold. Carey groaned.

"I just mopped out there."

"Mare," Enin said, in the doorway. Mare gave him a half-hearted smile. "Working hard?"

"Go away."

"No, don't!" Carey cried, halting him as he turned. "Peri, tell him what you said. About the magic. Peri said the chain is magic, so Mare said you must take it off with magic."

"And where," Enin asked, "do we find magic? Among the codfish in our nets?"

"Find someone who does magic. There are people who can."

He rubbed his beard silently, blinking at Carey as

41

she knelt among the suds. They had all stopped working, brushes suspended.

"A mage," he said. "A wizard."

"Yes!"

"We could offer gold. There's enough of it."

"Yes."

"With that kind of payment, we could get a good mage. The best. Someone who could break that chain and keep it from falling back down to the bottom of the sea."

"Someone who could keep you from killing yourselves over that gold," Mare said tartly.

His eyes moved to her. "Well," he admitted, "we have been a little carried away. But if you could see it, Mare, if you could—"

Peri shook her hair out of her eyes, suddenly uneasy. "Maybe you shouldn't," she said.

"Shouldn't what?"

"Disturb what's under the sea. Maybe the chain begins in a dangerous place."

They looked at her silently a moment, envisioning, amid the sea of suds, dangerous beginnings. Then Carey cried, "Oh, Peri, there's nothing to be afraid of!" The door opened again, slammed. Heavy boots stamped into the hall. Enin turned his head, cheerful again.

"Ami! We're going to get that gold!"

"How?"

"We're going to hire a magician!"

Magicians, Peri thought, huddling in her cloak as she walked down the beach. Kings. Sea-dragons. How, she wondered, had such words come to live in her head among plain familiar words like fish stew and scrub

42

bucket? She wiped rain out of her eyes. Gulls sailed the wind over her head, crying mournfully. Her fingers were almost numb in the cold. She carried mussels the innkeeper had given her bundled in a corner of her cloak. The cloak was beginning to smell like old seaweed. As soon as the rains stopped, she would . . .

She heard hoofbeats and peered into the rain. A riderless horse galloped down the beach toward her. Against the dusky sky, she could not see its eyes, just its black, black head and body, like a piece of polished night. There was a long strand of kelp caught on one hoof. It passed her; the tide ran in and out of its path.

She made a wordless noise. And then she began to run, not knowing exactly why or where. The darkening world seemed of only two colors: the deep gray of sky and stone and water, and the misty white of foam and gulls' wings. The mussels scattered as she ran. The wind whipped her hood back, tugged her hair loose. She saw the old woman's house finally; there was no fire in its windows, the door was closed. She slowed, her eyes searching the beach. She saw a streak of black in the tide, half in, half out of the sea. She ran again.

It was Kir, face down in the sand. She dropped to her knees beside him, rolled him onto his back. His face looked ghostly; she couldn't hear him breathe. She gripped both his hands and rose, trying to tug him out of the encroaching grip of the tide. She pulled once, twice. His clothes were weighted with water and sand; she could barely move him. She shifted her grip to his wrists and gave a mighty tug. He pulled against her, coming alive. Sea water spilled out of his mouth. She let him go; he curled onto his side, his body heaving for air. The rasping, grating breaths he took turned suddenly into sobbing. She felt her body prick with shock; her own eyes grew wide with unshed tears.

"I don't know what to do," she heard him cry. "I don't know what to do. What must I do? I belong to the sea and it will not let me in, and I cannot bear this land and it will not let me go."

"Oh," Peri whispered; hot tears slid down her face. "Oh." She knelt beside him again, put her arms around his back and shoulders, held him tightly, awkwardly. She felt the grit of sand in his hair against her cheek, smelled the sea in his clothing. The tide boiled up around them, ebbed slowly. "There must be a way, there must be, we'll find it," she said, hardly listening to herself. "I'll help you find the path into the sea, I promise, I promise. . . ."

She felt him quiet against her. He turned slowly, shakily, on his knees to face her. He put his arms around her wearily, his hands twined in her hair, his chilled face against her face. He did not speak again; he held her until the tide roared around them, between them, forcing them to choose between land and sea, to go, or stay forever.

Five

Enin and Tull were absent from the sea and the inn for several days. The other fishers, whose hours on the water were intermittent and dangerous, told one another tales of other, wilder storms they had survived and of the strangest things they had ever pulled up from the bottom of the sea. Now and then, as Peri passed them, she heard a brief mention of magic, of wizardry, followed by a sudden silence, as if they were all envisioning, over their beers, the wondrous, powerful mage whom Enin and Tull were at that very moment enticing out of the city. There was no more talk of gold now, lest the word seep under the door into the curious, greedy ears of the visitors. The fishers, gold within their grasp, waited.

Then, for a while, the village was overrun with some very peculiar people. Carey counted fourteen jugglers, six fortune-tellers, nine would-be alchemists who, she said tartly, couldn't even make change for a gold coin, four inept witches, and any number of tattered, impoverished wizards who couldn't unlatch a door by magic, let alone unlink a chain. The fishers gave them a dour reception; they, in their turn, saw no sign of gold or dragon in the bitter, tossing sea, and jeered the fishers for drunken dreamers. They all trailed back to the city; the fishers slumped over their beers, mocking Enin and Tull for their thickheadedness and still seeing their fortunes glittering somewhere beyond the spindrift.

Peri, lost so deeply in her own thoughts, had barely noticed the motley crowd from the city, except when she dodged a juggler's ball or tripped over a witch's skinny familiar. On the morning the storm finally passed, she barely noticed the silence. She scrubbed at an unfamiliar patch of sunlight as if it were one more puddle to clean off the flagstones. She was trying to imagine the world beneath the sea that Kir yearned for so desperately. Where could he have got to, that night, if he had found entry to the sea's cold heart? What would he change into? A creature of water and pearl, son of the restless tide . . . She scowled, scrubbing away at memories: his hands in her hair, the chill kiss on her cheek, his need of her, someone human to hold.

On land, at least she could touch him.

"Peri," Mare said, and Peri, startled, came up out of layer upon layer of thought. "You've been working on the same spot for twenty minutes. Are you trying to scrub through to the other side of the world?"

"Oh." She pushed her bucket and herself forward automatically. Mare, her feet in the way, did not move.

"Are you all right, girl?"

"I'm all right."

"You're so quiet lately."

"I'm all right," Peri said. Mare still didn't move.

46

"Growing pains," she decided finally, and her feet walked out of eyesight. "You finish the hall, then help me upstairs when you're done."

Peri grunted, shoved her bucket farther down the hall. The frown crept back over her face. The wave of suds she sent across the floor turned into tide and foam.

There was a sudden crash. The inn door, with someone clinging to it, had blown open under a vigorous puff of spring wind. Peri looked up to see a stranger lose his balance on her tide. He danced upright a moment, and she noticed finally the blazing thunderheads and the bright blue sky beyond him. Then he tossed his arms and fell, slid down the hall to kick over her bucket before he washed to a halt under her astonished face.

They stared at one another, nose to nose. The stranger lay prone, panting slightly. Peri, wordless, sat back on her knees, her brush, suspended, dripping on the stranger's hair.

The stranger smiled after a moment. He was a small, dark-haired, wiry young man with skin the light polished brown of a hazelnut. His eyes were very odd: a vivid blue-green-gray, like stones glittering different colors under the sun. He turned on his side on the wet floor and cupped his chin in his palm.

"Who are you?"

"Peri." She was so surprised that her voice nearly jumped out of her.

"Periwinkle? Like the flower?" he asked.

"Is there a flower?" His eyes kept making her want to look at them, put a color to them. But they eluded definition.

"Oh, yes," the stranger said. "A lovely blue flower."

"I thought they were only snails."

"Why," the stranger asked gravely, "would you be named after a snail?"

"Because I didn't know there were flowers," Peri said fuzzily.

"I see." His voice was at once deep and light, with none of the lilt of the coastal towns in it. He regarded her curiously, oblivious to the water seeping into his clothes. His body looked thin but muscular, his hands lean and strong, oddly capable, as if they could as easily tie a mooring knot as a bow in a ribbon. He was dressed very simply, but not like a fisher, not like a farmer, not like one of the king's followers, either, for his leather was scuffed and the fine wool cloak that had threatened to sail away with him on the wind was threaded with grass stains. He popped a soap bubble with one forefinger and added, "I heard a rumor that someone here needs a magician."

She nodded wearily, remembering the tattered fortune-tellers, the alchemists in their colorful, bedraggled robes. Then she drew a sudden breath, gazing again into the stranger's eyes. That, she felt, must explain their changing, the suggestion in them that they had witnessed other countries, marvels. He looked back at her without blinking. As she bent closer, searching for the marvels, a door opened somewhere at the far side of the world.

"Peri!"

She jumped. The stranger sighed, got slowly to his feet. He stood dripping under the amazed stare of the innkeeper.

"Good morning," he said. "I'm—"

"You're all wet!"

"I'm all wet. Yes." He ran a hand down his damp clothes, and the dripping stopped. The flagstones were suddenly dry, too. So was the puddle outside the door. "My name is Lyo. I'm a—"

"Yes," the innkeeper said. He bustled forward, clutched the magician's arm as if he might vanish like Peri's scrub water. "Yes. Indeed you are. Come this way, sir. Peri, go down to the kitchen and bring the gentleman some breakfast."

"I'm not hungry," said the magician.

"A beer?"

"No," the magician said inflexibly. "Just Peri." He added, at the innkeeper's silence, "I'll see that her work gets done."

"That may well be," the innkeeper said with sudden grimness. "But she's a good, innocent girl, and we've promised to pay you in gold and not in Periwinkles."

Peri shut her eyes tightly, wishing a flagstone would rise under her feet and carry her away. Then she heard Lyo's laugh, and saw the flush that had risen under his brown skin.

He held out his hands to the innkeeper; his wrists were bound together by a chain of gold. "I only want her to take me to see the sea-dragon."

The innkeeper swallowed, staring at the gold. The chain became a gold coin in the magician's palm. "I'll need a room."

"Yes, your lordship. Anything else? Anything at all."

"A boat."

"There's the *Sea Urchin*," Peri said dazedly. "But it needs oars."

The odd eyes glinted at her again, smiling, curious. "Why would a *Sea Urchin* not have oars?"

"It lost them when my father drowned."

He was silent a moment; he seemed to be listening to things she had not said. He touched her gently, led her outside. "Oars it shall have." She was still clutching her brush. He took it from her, turned it into a small blue flower. "This," he said, giving it back to her, "is a periwinkle."

The magician borrowed oars from no discernible place, stripped the barnacles from the *Sea Urchin*'s bottom with his hand, put his ear to its side to listen for leaks, and pronounced it seaworthy. He rowed easily out of the harbor into open sea, his lank hair curling in the spray, his face burning darker in the sunlight. A pair of seals leaped in graceful arches in and out of the swells; seabirds the color of foam circled the blue above their heads. The magician hailed the seals cheerfully, whistled to the birds, and stopped rowing completely once to let a jellyfish drift past the bow. He seemed delighted by the sea life, as if he had seen little of it, yet he rowed fearlessly farther than Peri had ever gone, out to where the very surface of the world was fluid and dangerous, where the sea was the ruling kingdom they trespassed upon in their tiny, fragile boats, and the life and beauty in it lay far beneath them, in places forbidden to their eyes.

Peri's thoughts drifted to Kir, another sea secret. She had made him a promise: to help him find his way out of the world, away from her. But where was the bridge between land and water, between air and the undersea? She pulled her thoughts about her like a cloak, sat huddled among them, stirring out of them finally to see the magician's eyes, now as bottle-green as the water, on her face.

She shifted, disconcerted, as if he could pick thoughts

like flowers out of her head. But he only asked worriedly, "What is it? Don't you like the sea?"

"No."

"Ah, I'm sorry. I shouldn't have asked you to come with me."

"It's not that," she said. "I don't mind being on it like this. I don't like what's under—" She stopped abruptly; he finished for her.

"What's under the sea." He sounded surprised. "What is under the sea besides kelp and whales and periwinkles?"

"Nothing," she mumbled, frightened suddenly at the thought of telling a sea tale that was as yet barely more than a secret in a king's heart.

"Then what are you—" He stopped himself, then, letting go of the oars to ruffle at his hair. The oars, upended, hung patiently in the air. "I see. It's a secret."

She nodded, staring at the oars. "Are you—are you rowing by magic?"

He looked affronted, while the *Sea Urchin's* bow skewed around toward land and the oars looked as if they were dipped in air. She laughed; the magician smiled again, pleased. He gripped the oars, brought them back down. "No, Periwinkle, I'm not rowing by magic, though my back and my shoulders and my hands are all shouting at me to get out and walk—"

"Can you do that?" she breathed. "Walk on the sea?"

"If I could, would I be blistering my hands with these oars? Besides, walking on the sea is very peculiar business, I've heard. You walk out of the world, you find yourself in strange countries, where words and sen-

51

tences grow solid, underwater, like the branches of coral, and you can read coral colonies the way, on land, you can read history.'' He laughed at her expression.

''Is it true?''

''I don't know. I've never been there.''

''Where?''

''To the country beneath the sea.'' He was silent, then, watching her, his eyes oddly somber. ''Why,'' he asked slowly, ''do you want to know about the country?''

She almost told him, for if he knew it, he might know the path to it. But it was not her secret, it was Kir's. ''I don't,'' she said brusquely. He only nodded, accepting that, if not, she sensed, believing it, and she had to resist the urge to tell him all over again.

''I can row awhile,'' she said instead. ''I have strong arms.'' She changed places with him, took the oars. The *Sea Urchin* skimmed easily over the first sluggish, heaving swell she dipped the oars into; surprised, she pulled at them again and felt she was rowing in a duck pond. Lyo had put a little magic into the oars, she realized, to help her, and he had not told her. And he had turned a snail into a flower.

He could break that chain.

''How did you get to be a magician?'' she asked curiously. ''Were you born that way? With your eyes already full of magic?''

He smiled, his eyes, facing the sun, full of light. ''Magic is like night, when you first encounter it.''

''Night?'' she said doubtfully. She skipped a beat with one oar and the *Sea Urchin* spun a half-circle.

''A vast black full of shapes . . .'' He trailed his fingers overboard and the *Sea Urchin* turned its bow toward the horizon again. "Slowly you learn to turn the dark into shapes, colors. . . . It's like a second dawn breaking over the world. You see something most people can't see and yet it seems clear as the nose on your face. That there's nothing in the world that doesn't possess its share of magic. Even an empty shell, a lump of lead, an old dead leaf—you look at them and learn to see, and then to use, and after a while you can't remember ever seeing the world any other way. Everything connects to something else. Like that gold chain connecting air and water. Where does it really begin? Above the sea? Below the sea? Who knows, at this point? When we find out, we'll never be able to look at the sea the same way again. Do you understand any of my babbling?"

Peri nodded. Then she shook her head. Then she flushed, thinking of the tipsy webs of black thread and twigs she had thrown into the sea. How could she have thought they held any power of magic? There was no more magic in her than in a broom. "Where?" she asked gruffly. "Where did you learn?" The magician's eyes were curious again, as if they were searching for those childish hexes in her head.

He opened his mouth to answer, and then didn't. His eyes had moved from her to a point over her shoulder; his hands moved, gripped the sides of the boat. His face had gone very still. She knew then what he was seeing. She pulled the oars out of the water into the boat, and turned.

The magician stood up. He balanced easily in the boat, under the great fiery stare of the sea-dragon. They were still a quarter of a mile from the fishing boats, but it had come to greet them, it seemed, lifting its bright barnacled head out of the water. Its body wavered beneath the surface of the water like a shifting flame.

Lyo whistled. The sea-dragon's brow fins twitched at the noise. *"Ignus Dracus,"* the magician murmured. "The firedragon of the Southern Sea. It appears to be lost. No . . ." He was silent again, frowning. The firedragon watched him. The chain around its neck was blinding in the noon light.

The magician sat down again slowly. His face was an unusual color, probably, Peri thought, from the gold; everything around them was awash with gold. The fishers were hauling in their nets. They knew the *Sea Urchin*, and they knew that only something momentous would send Peri that far out in it.

Peri felt a sudden surge of excitement at the imminence of magic. "Can you break that chain?"

He looked at her without seeing her. "The chain," he said finally. "Oh, yes. The chain is simple."

"Really?"

"It's just—" He waved a hand, oddly inarticulate. "There are just a couple of—Did anyone ever think to ask where this chain begins? Who made it and why?"

"Yes."

"Well?"

She shrugged, avoiding his eye. "They want the gold."

"The king? Did he see it?"

Peri stared at him. He was troubled; the colors in his eyes shifted darkly. Kir, she thought, and as she tried to hide the thought, his words came back to her: *The chain begins in my father's heart.* But his secret was not hers to give away. "No," she said briefly. His face stilled again; he watched her. How did he know? she wondered, rowing a little to keep the *Sea Urchin* from drifting. How did he know to ask that?

"Peri," he said softly. "Sometimes two great kingdoms that should exist in different times, on different planes, become entangled with one another. Tales begin there. Songs are sung, names remembered. . . . This is not the first time.''

She looked away from the magician again, letting the wind blow her hair across her face, hide her from his magic eyes. Kir, his blood trying to ebb with the ebb tide, the secret pain, the secret need in his eyes . . .

"Just break the chain," she pleaded.

"And then what?"

"I don't know. . . ." She added, "We'll pay you."

He studied her for a long time, while the fishing boats inched closer around them. "It's just the gold you want then."

She nodded, her eyes on a passing gull. "So we'll be rich. You'll be rich, too," she reminded him, and he made an odd noise in his throat.

"I'll do my best," he said gravely, "to make us all rich." He stood up again, then, and began to sing to the sea-dragon.

The boats gathered about the *Sea Urchin* as he sang. The sea-dragon's big, round eyes never moved from him. Birds landed on its head, dove for the fish that followed it constantly; it never moved. Swells nearly heaved the magician overboard a couple of times; he only shifted his feet as if he had been born in a boat and never left it. His songs were in strange languages; the words and tunes wove eerily into the wind and waves and the cries of the birds. The fishers waited silently, plying oars now and then to keep from running into one another, for the bottom dropped away from the world where they floated and there was nothing but darkness to anchor in.

Gradually the songs became comprehensible. They

were, Peri realized with astonishment, children's songs. Songs to teach sounds, letters, words, the noises of animals. The fishers glanced at one another dubiously. The sea-dragon drifted closer; its eyes loomed in front of the *Sea Urchin* like round red doors.

The magician stopped finally, hoarse and sweating. He poured himself a beer out of nowhere, and the fishers grinned. This was no flea-bitten fortune-teller.

"My name," he said, "is Lyo. This, we'll assume for the moment, is a species of *Ignus Dracus*, which originated in the warm, light-filled waters of the Southern Sea, where kelp and brine shrimp abound. This one apparently muddled into the vast, slow-moving maelstrom formed by the south current as it shifts upward to meet the cold northeast current, which circles downward in its turn to meet the warm south currents again on the other side of the sea." He paused to sip beer. The fishers listened respectfully. Some had even taken off their hats. "It got lost, in other words, which is, we'll also assume for the moment, what it's doing here. The chain, however, is not a normal feature of *Ignus Dracus*. It is not a normal feature of anything I have ever laid eyes on in the sea. I will remove it for you. For a small fee, of course. A nominal fee. A quarter-weight of the salvaged chain."

They spoke then, jamming hats back on their heads. "A quarter of the gold! That's—that's—"

"At this point, a quarter of nothing."

"That's robbery!"

"No," Lyo said cheerfully. "Simple greed. I like gold. Take it or leave it. Remember: Three or four links alone will be enough to make the town rich. I can get you far more than that."

56

There was silence. "One link," someone growled. "One link is yours. The rest ours."

Peri laid her arms along the side of the boat and rested her chin on them, watching the sea-dragon. It seemed to enjoy the bargaining: Its head turned ponderously at every new voice. What was it really? she wondered. What had the magician seen within its great, calm eyes? Something to do with Kir?

How had the magician known?

"All right," she heard him say finally. "The first link, and then one out of every five mine. Are we agreed?" He waited; a sea gull made a rude noise above his head. "Good. Now . . . just keep quiet for a couple of minutes, that's all I need. Just . . . silence. . . ."

The *Sea Urchin* was inching toward the sea-dragon. The drift looked effortless, but it was against the tide, and Peri could see the drag of Lyo's magic at his back. He was frowning deeply; his face seemed blanched beneath its tan. The sea-dragon's eyes were dead ahead, twin portals of constant fire the *Sea Urchin* seemed determined to enter. The magician's eyes burned like jewels in the bright reflection of the gold.

The boat bumped lightly against the chain. There was not a sound around them, not even from the gulls. Lyo leaned forward, laid a palm on the massive, glowing chain. His hand and face seemed transformed: He wore a gauntlet and a mask of gold.

And then the gold was gone. Peri blinked, and blinked again. It was as if the sun had vanished out of the sky. The sea-dragon made a sound, a quick, timbreless bellow. Then its head ducked down and it was gone.

All around the boats floated thousands upon thousands of periwinkles.

Six

"Oops," was all the magician said about it before he vanished. "Sorry." A fisher from one of the larger boats rowed Peri in; he was glumly silent all the way until he slewed the *Sea Urchin* into its berth in the placid harbor. Then he spat into the water.

"There are some men born to be magicians. And some magicians born to be fish bait." He heaved himself out of the boat, headed toward the inn.

Peri tied up the *Sea Urchin*, then stood a moment, feeling blank, a vast blue haze of periwinkles floating in her head. No more gold, the sea-dragon gone. . . .

"Periwinkles." Her own voice startled her. She walked down the dock toward the inn, then veered away from it. She had no desire to hear Carey's thoughts on the matter of gold turned into flowers. There would be days enough ahead for that. Months, likely. Where, she wondered, had the magician gone?

Where had the sea-dragon and the gold gone? Where

all the moonlit paths to the country beneath the sea always went? To that elusive land called memory?

She sighed. In the bright, blustery afternoon, all the magic had fled, just when she had begun to believe it existed. And now, voices caught her ear from across the harbor, where the king's lovely fleet ships were docked.

She stopped, staring. Sailors were scouring one of the ships, whistling; others loaded chests, white hens in cages. . . .

Someone else was leaving.

She felt her eyes ache suddenly. She twisted her hair in her hands, away from her face. "Well," she said to herself, her voice so swollen and deep it didn't seem to belong to her, "what did you expect?" A horse returning riderless, a prince coming home half-drowned in the sea—even an absentminded father would pay attention to that.

She dragged her eyes away from the ship, herself away from the harbor. She wandered through the village with its distant afternoon sounds of women chatting across walls as they worked in their vegetable gardens, children playing in the trees, calling to one another. Her rambling took her, as always, to her mother's gate. The hoe was still standing in the weeds. She stopped, glaring at it. Where were the furrows, the seeds for spring? Her mother had to eat.

She grabbed the hoe, ignoring the pale, listless face at the window, and attacked the rain-soaked ground.

Several hours later, she sat on the wall, dirty, sweating, aching, and surveyed her work. There were mud streaks even in her hair. A great pile of weeds lay to one side of the garden; the dark, turned path in the middle was ready for potatoes, cabbages, carrots, squash. The sun was lowering behind her, filling the yard with a mellow light. A sweet sea breeze cooled her face. She ignored the sea for a while, then gave up, turned to it. The boats were homing toward the harbor on a streak of silver fire.

She gazed at it, her heart aching again. She felt a touch on her shoulder; her mother stood beside her. They both watched silently. Peri's tangled head came to rest against her mother's shoulder. The sea, it seemed, had lured them both into its dreaming. Maybe there was no way out of the dream; they would be caught in it forever, yearning for a secret that was never quite real, never quite false. . . .

"Well." She stirred from the wall.

Her mother said softly, "Come in and eat, Peri."

She shook her head. "I'm not hungry. Get some seeds. I'll come and plant them."

"At least," her mother said in a more familiar tone, "wash before you go."

Peri drew water from the rain barrel, poured it over her hair and arms and feet until she was clean and half-drowned. She shook her soaked hair over her shoulders and drifted back out of the yard, through the village, to the beach. She followed the tide line, not looking at the sea except once: when she neared the spires and lifted her head to see the blinding light sinking down between them, showering its gold over empty waters.

She ducked her head again, trudged to the old woman's house. She opened the door, and found Kir, sitting on a stool with his feet on the window ledge, watching the sun go down.

He rose, went to her as she stopped in the doorway.

He put his arms around her wordlessly; after a moment her hands rose shyly, touched his back. She closed her eyes against the light, felt him stroke her hair.

"You're wet," he commented, "this time."

"I was gardening."

"Oh." She felt him draw a long breath, loose it. Then he loosed her slowly, looking at her with his strange, clear, relentless gaze. "I'm leaving for a while."

"I know," she whispered. "I saw the ship."

"My father—" He stopped, a muscle working in his jaw. "My father is taking me to visit a lord and lady in the North Isles. They have a daughter."

"Oh."

"I'll be back."

"How do you know?"

His eyes left her, strayed toward the final, shivering path of light across the sea. "You know why," he whispered. "You know." His lips brushed hers, cold, yet she knew he gave her all the warmth he had. "If I could love, I would love you," he said softly. After a moment she smiled. "Why is that strange?"

"If you could love," she said simply, feeling as if she had taken an enormous step away from herself, and into the complex world, "you would not choose me to love."

He was silent. She moved away from him, sat down tiredly, and was instantly sorry that he was no longer close to her. He paced the room a little, looking out. Then he stopped behind her, put his arms around her again, held her tightly, his face burrowed into her hair. She took his hands in her hands, lifted them to her face. She said, "Promise me."

"What?"

"Stay safe, where you're going. Don't drown."

She felt his head shake quickly. "No. I wasn't trying to, that night. I was swimming beyond the spires, trying to follow the light. But the faster I swam, the farther it drew from me; I followed it until it was gone, and I was alone in the deep water, in the darkening sea. . . . I think—I think for the first time that night my father—the thought occurred to my father whose child I might be. I saw him look at me with changed eyes. Eyes that saw me for a moment. He does not want to believe it." He paused; she felt his heartbeat. "That night you pulled me out of the sea . . . before that night, I had never cried. Not even as a child. Not true tears. You made me remember I am half human." He moved to face her as she sat mute; he knelt, lifted her hands to his mouth. She drew a breath, felt herself pulled toward him helplessly, thoughtlessly. Something fiery brushed her closed eyes, her mouth; she lifted her face to it. But it was only the last finger of light from the setting sun.

Kir had moved to the window. She sat back, blinking, watching him watch the tide withdraw. Then, before she could feel anything—love, loss, sorrow—he looked down at her again. You know me, his eyes said. You know what I am. Nothing less. Nothing more.

She got up finally, took bread out of the cupboard, butter, a knife. "I'm lucky," she said, and heard her voice tremble.

"Why?"

She turned to look at him again, his hair black against the dusk, his eyes shades of blue darker than the dusk. She swallowed. "That you are only half like your mother," she whispered. "Because it would be very hard to say no to the sea."

His eyes changed, no longer the sea's eyes. He went to her, his head bent; he took the butter knife out of her hand, held her hand to his cheek. "Yes," he said huskily. "You are lucky. Because I would rise out of the tide bringing you coral and black pearls, and I would not rest until I had your heart, and that I would carry away with me back into the sea, and leave you, like me, standing on a barren shore, crying for what the sea possessed, and with no way but one to get it." He loosed her hand, kissed her cheek swiftly, not letting her see his eyes. "I must go. We're sailing on the outgoing tide. I'll be back."

He left her. The house seemed suddenly too still, empty. She sat down at the table, her eyes wide, her body still, feeling him, step by step, carrying away her heart.

She stood at the open door hours later, watching the moon wander through an indigo sky, watching the path it made across the sea constantly break apart and mend itself: the road into dreams, into the summer isles. She listened to the sea breathe, heard Kir's breathing in her memories. A tear ran down her cheek, surprising her.

"What have you done?" she asked herself aloud. "What have you done?" She answered herself a few moments later. "I've gone and fallen in love with the sea."

"I thought so," said a shadow beside her doorstep, and she felt her skin prickle like a sea urchin's.

"Lyo!"

He moved out of the shadow, or else ceased being one. The moonlight winked here and there on him in unexpected places; he smelled of sage and broom where he must have been lying earlier.

"Where did you go?" she demanded amazedly.

"Up the cliff."

"How? How did you get there from the *Sea Urchin* on open sea?"

"As quickly as possible." She saw one side of his mouth curve upward in a thin, slanted smile. Then, as abruptly, he stopped smiling; his face was a pale mask in the moonlight, his eyes pools of shadow. "More easily than you left the sea."

She was silent. She gave up trying to see his eyes and sat down on the step, chewed on a thumbnail. Then she wound her hair into a knot at the back of her neck and let it fall again. "I thought I had more sense," she said finally. "Do you know what being in love is like?"

"Yes."

"It's like having a swarm of gnats inside you."

"Oh."

"They won't be still, and they won't go away. . . . What are you doing here? I thought you ran away."

He chuckled softly. "I'm waiting to be paid." He sat down beside her; she felt his fingers, light as moth wings, brush her cheek. "You were crying. It's a terrible thing, loving the sea."

"Yes," she whispered, her eyes straying to it. Waves gathered and broke invisibly in the dark, reaching toward her, pulling back. They were never silent, they never spoke. . . . Then she looked at the magician out of the corners of her eyes. "You know about Kir."

"I know."

"How? How could you know something like that?"

He reached down, picked up a glittering pebble beside his feet and flicked it absently seaward. "I listen," he said obscurely. "If you listen hard enough, you begin to hear things . . . the sorrow beneath the smile, the voice within the firedragon, the secret in the young floor-scrubber's voice, behind all the talk of gold. . . ."

"Gold," she said morosely, reminded. "Don't let the fishers see you still here."

"I won't."

"At least you tried. At least you showed them some magic."

"Perhaps," he said, chuckling again. "I won't expect to be overwhelmed by their thanks. But, not only can I turn gold into periwinkles, I can think as well. And what I think is this: There's someone missing."

"What do you mean?"

"There's Kir. There's his father, the king. There are two wives. Suppose this: Suppose they bore sons of the king at the same time. The son of the land-born queen was stolen away at birth and a changeling—a child of the sea—was slipped into his place. The queen died. But what happened to her true son? Kir's half-brother."

She was silent, trying to imagine a shadowy reflection of Kir. A shiver rippled through her. Somewhere in the night, a king's child wandered nameless, heir to the world Kir so desperately wished to leave. "Maybe he died."

"Perhaps. But I think he lived. I think he's living now, the only proof of the king's secret love. Does Kir suspect he might have a brother?"

She shook her head wearily. "He hasn't thought that far yet. He's barely guessed what he is, himself."

"Why did he tell you?" the magician asked curiously.

"I don't know. Because I was always thinking about the sea and so was he. Because . . ." Her voice trailed away; she put her face on her arms, swallowing drily.

"He almost drowned one evening. I pulled him out of the surf. Another evening, he left wet footprints all over the house. Because he needed someone to tell, and I was here instead of the old woman. Because I work at the inn, and he can come and go in and out of my house, and no one would even think to look for him here. A few weeks ago all I did was scrub floors. I don't know how things got so complicated.''

"They do sometimes when you're not paying attention. Will you let me help you both?''

"It's all right for now. He's going away to meet some lord's daughter.''

"He'll be back.''

"I almost wish he wouldn't. I almost wish he would sail away as far as he could sail, across all the days and nights there are to the end of the sea, and never come back.'' She saw Kir's face in the dark, dark sea, felt his touch, luring her out into deep water with cold kisses and promises of sea-flowers and pearls; she saw him again, crying in the surf, clinging to her on land, as she would have clung to him in the sea.

Her eyes had filled again with tears at the memory of his sorrow. Lyo said again, gently, "Will you let me help?''

"Yes,'' she whispered. "But be careful. You must always be careful of the sea.''

She still watched, long after Lyo had left her. The moon was over the dunes now, queen of the fishes in a starry sea. The tide had quieted; the long, slow breakers whispered to her of magic hidden in that blackness: the great floating islands drifted past just beyond eyesight, the ivory towers on them spiraled and pointed like the narwhale's horn. Kir's world, the world his heart hungered for, elusive as moonlight, as water, yet constantly calling . . . She felt the touch of his lean, tense hands, saw his sea eyes, seeing her as nobody else did, heard his voice saying her name.

"Oh," she whispered, her throat aching, the stars blurring in her eyes. "I wish you were human." She blinked away tears after a moment. "No," she sighed, speaking to the waves since she had nothing else of Kir. "If you were human, you would never have given me a thought. A girl who works at the inn. You would never even have known my name. I wish—I just wish you were a little bit more human. So that you wouldn't always be turning away from me to the sea."

Something moved within the darkness. It flowed across her vision until it blotted out one star, and then another. Her skin prickled again; her eyes grew wide as she tried to separate dark from dark. Was it the sea country rising from the depths of the sea? Was it some dream island that shifted by night from place to place? Was it some vast, dark, high-riding wave? But the receding waves broke evenly, serenely against the shore. Still the darkness flowed until, by the outline of black against the stars and the foam, she realized what it was.

She stood up slowly. The sea-dragon was riding on the surf, closer to land than she had ever seen it. Lyo had freed it, yet it lingered, alone in the night, missing the fishers. Had it been drawn by her lamplight? She found herself moving quickly, impulsively across the sand, drawn toward it, trying to see it more clearly. It swallowed more stars. One of the spires disappeared behind its back, then the other. Her feet dragged abruptly in the sand, stopped.

It was coming out of the sea.

Her throat made a whimpering noise, but she was frozen, incapable of moving. She could see the great eyes reflecting moonlight, the mountain of its back, the enormous fins along its body pushing it through the shallow water into the tide. "Lyo," she said, but as in a dream, her voice had no sound. Was it coming out to die, she wondered, like the whales did sometimes? Or was it just coming out like the sea lions came out, to stretch its great body on the dry sand and sleep?

It was coming straight toward her; its fiery eyes saw her. She stepped back; it gave a mournful cry like a foghorn, and she stood still again. It can't eat me, she thought wildly. It could roll on me, but I can move faster. What does it want?

Its back fins heaved the bulk of it out of the surf. The tide played with its streamers awhile, rolled them up, stretched them out, delicate ribbons of smoke. Still it came, heave by heave, until only the long, tapering tail fin was left in the surf, and finally only its tail streamers.

And then it was all out, one final streamer tugged out of reach of the tide. And not six yards from her. Her hands were jammed over her mouth; she was poised to scream, to run all the way to the village if it decided to sit on her house. But it stopped heaving, stopped moving completely except for a whuff of a huge sigh out of its mouth.

Its eyes closed, red moons vanishing. And then all of it vanished.

A young man, naked as a fish, knelt on his hands and knees at the end of the path the sea-dragon had taken out of the sea.

Seven

Peri made a noise. She still had her hands over her mouth, so it was a muffled noise. The sea-dragon's head lifted. He stared at her groggily, blinking, the salt water dripping from his hair into his eyes. He shook his head wildly, and stared at her again. She stood like one of the stone spires, like something to which barnacles and sea urchins could drift against and cling. But he did not confuse her with a stone. He turned his head to look at the stars, the waves, the sand, and finally his hands.

He touched his mouth with one hand. He said rapidly, experimentally, "One fish sat on a house, two fish ate a mouse, three fish—" His voice faltered. "Three fish . . . three fish . . ." He looked frightened, then desperate, as if he had forgotten some vital magic spell that was the lifeline to his new body. His eyes went back to Peri. She moved her hands after a moment; her bones felt brittle, like dried coral.

"Three fish rode a horse." Her voice seemed to come

from somewhere else, out of the well under the gorse, perhaps. Her heart thumped raggedly. She felt as if she had stepped into some dream where anything might happen: Her head might float away and turn into the moon; starfish might walk upright onto the sand and dance a courtly dance.

The terror went out of the sea-dragon's face.

"Three fish rode a horse. Four fish swam in the gorse." It was one of the children's rhymes Lyo had chanted to the sea-dragon. "Five fish climbed a bee." The sea-dragon was beginning to shiver.

"A tree," Peri said numbly. "Five fish climbed a tree."

"Six fish caught a bee."

She took a step toward him, breaking out of the spell he was weaving about them both with his rhyming. "You're cold." He was silent at the unfamiliar word, watching her. In that moment, with his face still, up-lifted to the moonlight, his hair dark with water, he looked eerily like Kir.

She closed her eyes, suddenly chilled herself. The king's missing son. He had crawled out of the sea, found his body and his voice and was kneeling stark naked under the stars counting fish in front of her.

"Seven fish dined with the king." His voice sounded strained again, uneasy at her silence. "Eight fish found a ring. Nine fish—"

Peri took another step toward him and he stopped speaking. She moved again and he stopped breathing. This time he was frozen in the sand, watching her come.

She reached him finally. He slid back on his knees to look up at her. His face, lit by the moon above the dunes, seemed unafraid. In his great, bulky underwater body, he would never have learned fear. Her hand moved of its own accord, another piece of the dream, and touched his shoulder.

At her touch, he began to breathe again. His skin was icy. He still watched her, his face curious, very calm. But when she lifted her hand, something flickered in his eyes; he put his own hand where hers had been.

She shivered again, glimpsing the complex, mysterious events that had hidden this king's son behind those huge, inhuman eyes, in that body with streamers for fingers, fins for feet, and the rest of him home for any passing barnacle. "Down in the sea," she whispered, "did anyone ever touch you? How could—how could anyone do such things to you and Kir? What makes people do such things?"

He was listening, as the sea-dragon had listened, alert for every pitch and shading in her voice. He picked up a word unexpectedly, hearing an overtone.

"Kir."

She swept at her hair with both hands, utterly perplexed. "I should take you to the king," she said, and was horrified at the thought. "I can't walk into his great house with you in the middle of the night and explain to him—me, Peri, who mops floors at the inn—that you are his human son and Kir is his sea-child and—I can't, anyway," she added with vast relief. "He left with Kir. Lyo. Lyo can tell me what to do with you." The sea-dragon was listening patiently, his teeth chattering. She put her arm around him, coaxing him to his feet. "At least I can find you a blanket. Can you walk? Not very well, but no wonder, you just got born."

She took him into the house, wrapped him in an old quilt and rekindled the fire under a pot of oyster soup.

The light springing over his face made her eyes widen. His hair was as gold as the sea-dragon's chain; his eyes were sky blue under gold brows. Like Kir, he was tall, slender, broad-shouldered; like the sea-dragon, he was constantly in motion. He paced while he nibbled bread. He burned his fingers in the fire, poked himself with a needle, startled himself with the cracked mirror, tripped over the trailing quilt, and dropped everything he picked up, including his bread and a bowl of oyster soup. Peri made him sit down finally, curled his fingers around a spoon and taught him to feed himself. The first spoonful of hot milk, oysters, melted butter, salt, and pepper he swallowed amazed him. Peri laughed at his expression. An answering smile sprang to his face, mirroring hers. It was a smile startlingly unlike Kir's, sweet and free of bitterness. She gazed at him, silent again, forgetting to eat. He waited, alert to her silence, as curious and patient as the sea-dragon had been, balancing its lumbering body in the waves among the fishers' boats to listen to them talk.

"I wonder if you even have a name," she breathed finally. "I wonder what your mother called you, just before she died. You must look like her. I wonder if, down in the sea, they ever took off the chain, turned you back into this shape. . . . I wonder if they ever taught you anything at all, even 'yes' and 'no.' "

"Yes and no," the sea-dragon said obligingly, "and dark and light, sun and moon and day and night: They never speak, but to and fro together through the world they go."

"Or did they just keep you chained from the day they took you? Is this really the first time you have been human?"

72

"Human."

"Like me. Like the fishers."

He let the bowl sag forward in his hands as he listened, his eyes intent on her eyes, her mouth. His own eyes were heavy; the sea-dragon's struggle out of the sea had tired him. She righted the bowl before he spilled it, coaxed him to eat more soup before he nodded away and tumbled off his chair. She made him lie on a blanket beside the hearth; he was asleep, soundlessly, before she covered him.

She stood watching the firelight lay protective arms across him. Twice in one day, she thought; two princes have come into my house. One dark, one light, one day, one night. . . . And then she fell into bed without getting undressed.

She woke again in the dark to the roar of the high tide. A puddle of moonlight splashed through her open door. It creaked as she stared at it, then banged shut making her jump.

The blankets lay scattered, empty beside the hearth. She was alone. She got out of bed, went to the window. The milky, moonlit sea dazzled her eyes; she leaned farther out, blinking, and saw it finally: the sea-dragon with all its streamers swirling about it taking the silver path of light between the spires, back into the sea.

She worked groggily at the inn that day. Carey, bewailing the loss of the gold unceasingly, it seemed, became to Peri's ears like a background noise of shrill, keening gulls' voices. Even Mare, with all her good sense and humor, was cross.

"How could he have been so stupid?" Carey demanded. "How could anyone with the power to turn gold into anything at all have turned it into a bunch of flowers? All that gold, Mare. . . . Peri, you were with him. Did you have any idea he would do anything so barnacle-brained as that?''

Peri shook her head and swallowed a yawn. Carey stood in front of her, wanting something, some word of explanation, of hope. When none came, she made a desperate noise and stared out a window.

''I'm going to run away.''

''Oh, please,'' Mare sighed. ''Stop caterwauling about the gold. It's gone. We've lived our lives so far without it, and if just living peacefully won't make you happy, I don't suppose a fortune will, either.''

''You're sorry about it, too.''

''All right, so I am. It would be fine not to have to scrub floors and listen to you complain every day; if you're going to go, then go for goodness sake, girl, and give us a rest.''

''All right, then,'' Carey snapped. Peri lifted her head. Something in the tense, poised lines of Carey's body reminded Peri of Kir's desperation and helpless anger.

''Don't go,'' she said softly. Carey's miserable, furious gaze swung to her. ''Maybe he'll be back. He has magic in him. He had the power.''

The anger vanished from Carey's face. She went to Peri, grabbed her broom to keep it still. ''Yes. You're right. If he could turn gold into flowers, why can't he turn the flowers back into gold? He could, couldn't he? If we could find him, if we could ask him.''

''Those flowers are probably down in the south islands by now,'' Mare said. ''And so, if he knows what's good for him, is the magician. You heard the fishers

74

yesterday when they came in. If the magician had been anywhere within reach, they would have corked him into a beer barrel and tossed him back out to sea."

"But—" Carey said stubbornly.

"What?"

"The magic was real. It was real, Mare. Peri is right. He has the power."

Mare was silent, frowning uncertainly. Peri closed her eyes a moment, wishing she could curl up under a table and take a nap. An image of the sea-dragon exuberantly breasting the moonlit waves swam into her head. Yes and no and dark and light, his voice said, just as her head nodded forward against her broom and snapped back up again.

"Peri!" Mare exclaimed. "You're falling asleep!"

"Sorry."

"What have you been doing at night, girl? Meeting phantom lovers?"

"Yes," she said yawning again. Unexpectedly, Carey laughed.

Peri's house was empty when she came home that afternoon. She ate bread and cheese beside the hearth, then crawled gratefully into bed before the sun went down. She slept deeply without dreaming; when she floated drowsily awake again, she wondered why it was still dark.

Someone was moving in the house. "Kir?" she said sleepily. "Lyo?" Then she came fully awake, for the door stood open and the bright moon hung like a lantern over her threshold.

A hand brushed her lightly. "Two fine ladies rode to town, in a carriage of seashells pulled by a prawn."

"You're back!"

"You're back," he echoed. He had already pulled a quilt over his shoulders; he was rubbing his dripping hair with a corner of it. "Peri," he added, and she started.

"Who taught you that?"

He burrowed more deeply into the quilt, then held out his hands to her cold hearth. Peri got out of bed. The fire she built chased away the fog in her head along with the darkness.

"Lyo," she exclaimed as the sea-dragon knelt to warm himself. "Has he been with you in the sea?"

He touched his mouth, feeling for words. Then he said in an arrogant, scholarly voice, "A species of *Ignus Dracus*, which originated in the warm, light-filled waters of the Southern Sea—oops, sorry."

She smiled wonderingly. "Is that how you turned human? If so, his spell last night didn't work too well; maybe tonight you'll stay human. But—" A frown crept into her eyes. She stopped the curious sea-dragon from putting her hairbrush on the fire. "But all I can teach you are words," she said, groping with words herself to say what she meant. "How will you know what they mean? How can you say where you've been? What you want?"

"Want is empty, have is full," he said. "Want is hungry—"

She turned; he stopped talking. But something in his eyes spoke, insisted, that when she taught him the language, he would have more to tell her than of kelp and shrimp and children's rhymes. He put his hands around his neck suddenly.

"Chain," he told her. "Chain." And she saw the human feeling in his eyes.

She took his hands, held them toward the blaze. "This is fire," she said.

"Fire."

She tugged him up, led him to the open door. "Those are stars. That is the moon."

"Stars. Moon."

"Sand," she said, pointing to it. "Sea."

"Sand." He fell silent, gazing out at the restless tide. "Sea," he whispered, and as she led him in, she wondered if the sudden wash of fire across his eyes had hidden love or hate.

He roamed the house, touching everything, remembering many of the words she told him. Finally he turned to her with the same scrutiny, touched her tangled hair.

"Hair," she said.

"Hair." He bent slightly, peering into her eyes, then at her nose with such intensity that she laughed. He startled, ducking back as gracefully as a fish. Then he smiled.

"Nose."

"Nose."

"Eyes."

"Eyes." He stared into hers again; even his lashes were gold, she saw, against a milky skin that had never been touched by the sun. She drew a breath, pulled herself out of his summer-blue gaze, and called his attention to the floor.

"Feet."

He grew drowsy soon; it taxed his strength, she

guessed, to heave that sea-body onto dry land. But before he fell asleep beside the fire, he told her a story.

"Once upon a time," he said in Lyo's voice, "There was a king who had two sons: one by the young queen, his wife, and one by a woman out of the sea. The sons were born at the same time, and when the queen died in childbed, her human son was stolen away, and the sea-born son left in his place. Why? No one truly knows, only the woman hidden in the sea, and the king. And perhaps the king does not even know. Why?

"Why is the wind, why is the sea, why is a long road between the world and me." He fell silent, watched the changing expressions on her face. He reached out, put his hand on her hand, and went to sleep.

When she woke in the morning, he was gone.

She went to work, puzzled. She searched for signs of the sea-dragon as she walked to the inn that morning, and again in the afternoon when she walked back. She cooked potatoes and sausages for supper, leaving her door open to catch the mild spring breeze. A shadow fell over her frying pan from the doorway; she whirled, and found the magician leaning against the doorpost.

"Lyo!"

He smiled. "I kept smelling something wonderful. I followed my nose." He looked thinner, she thought, and wondered what and where he ate. Certainly nowhere in the village. She took the pan off the flame and held it out to him. He took a smoking hot piece of potato, juggled it between his fingers, then bit into it and sighed.

"It's so good it must be magic."

"Lyo, where is the sea-dragon?"

"In the sea," he said with his mouth full. She gazed

at him, perplexed; he took a sausage from the pan. She sucked at a tine of her stirring fork.

"Well, why?" she said. "Can't you make a spell work right for once?"

He raised his brows at her, speechless as he bit into the sausage. "What," he said when he could finally speak, "are you asking?"

"I'm asking why you can't change the sea-dragon into a prince for more than a couple of hours at a time."

"Why can't—"

"First you change gold into flowers, then you change the sea-dragon, only you—"

"I didn't."

"You didn't change him?"

He shook his head, reaching for the pan again. She set it down finally on the table; they sat down, nibbled out of it, he with his fingers, she with the oversized fork.

"Then who did?"

He shook his head, looking as curious and as baffled as she felt. "I have no idea. It doesn't make any sense. That's really what I came to ask you."

"Me?"

"If you knew why it—he—changed so suddenly. And at such an odd time. Did you see anyone? Hear anything?"

She shook her head. "I was there when it happened; I was still watching the sea. It just crawled out. There was no magic. It just changed. He. Lyo." She paused, groping while he waited. "He is so—so—"

"His mother," Lyo said, finding another sausage, "was said to be very beautiful."

"Then why did the king love a sea-woman? If he had a wife like that?"

"Well." He chewed a moment, thoughtfully. "As I have heard, they barely knew each other before they were married. The king knew the sea-woman longer than that, I suspect. I think she was not a passing fancy, but someone who came to love him. The king didn't realize he would come to love his own wife as well. He married and forgot about the sea-woman, but he saw her one last time just before he married. And that was one time too many. Nine months later the queen was dead, her child taken under the sea, and the changeling cried in the royal cradle instead."

"It is sad."

"It is."

"The sea-dragon doesn't even have a name." She poked holes in the potatoes with the fork, brooding, while Lyo watched her, his eyes sometimes smiling, sometimes secret. "I wish the king and Kir would come back. Then—oh." She put the fork down. "What will Kir say? He doesn't have a home on land or sea; the sea-dragon is only human in the middle of the night—"

"It's an odd pair of sons for a king to have."

"Lyo, you have to do something."

"I am." He bent over the pan again. "I'm going to finish your supper."

The magician taught the sea-dragon in the sea by day; by night it crawled out of the sea to tell Peri the words it had learned, and to learn more from her. Peri, keeping such odd hours, felt life begin to muddle like a dream. She found herself mumbling "scrub brush" and "soap" as she sloshed water across the floor at the inn, and stray bits of children's rhymes ran constantly through her head. She saw little of Lyo; she assumed he slept at night, along with everybody else who lived their lives oblivious of the double life of sea-dragons. The ship that had carried Kir away remained stubbornly away.

"I heard," Carey said, full of gossip one morning as they began to work, "that the king took Kir up to the North Isles to marry some lord's daughter."

A huge soap bubble, rainbows trembling in it, fascinated Peri. She stared at it and tried to imagine Kir married. Like a breath of dark wind, something of his own frustration and panic blew through her. He might marry, but he would never love, and then there would be yet another child trapped in one world, yearning for another. And another young woman cruelly betrayed by the sea. She sighed. The bubble popped. The story would go on and on. . . .

Marc tripped over her feet. "I'm sorry, Peri. Where did you hear that?" she asked Carey.

"From one of the girls who works in the kitchen. She was bringing supper to some of the guests and heard them talking. They said Kir was restless and unhappy. The king thought marriage would settle him."

"Poor Kir," Mare said, and Peri looked up from the hearth she was cleaning.

"Why?"

"There's no magic in marriage. If they become friends, though, that would be different. But royal folk rarely get to marry their friends. They have to marry power or wealth or land or—"

"Well," Carey said wistfully, "at least they have that."

"Oh, Carey!" Mare said, laughing. "You're impossible."

"I can't help it," Carey said stubbornly. "I want to be rich. I want that sea-dragon's gold. Then I'll be happy."

Peri cooked supper for herself, and crawled into bed as soon as the sun set. The sea-dragon woke her out of her dreams to the roar of the sea, the wind shaking her door, the little barque of the moon sailing among scudding clouds. "Saucepan," she taught him. "Wall, fork, bread, salt." When her house held no more new words, she taught him sentences. "I am hungry. I am thirsty. Where are you? I am here. What are you doing? I am stirring onions in a pan, I am combing my hair. . . ." As the nights passed and the sea-dragon consumed words like shrimp, they made the sentences into a game.

"What are you doing?" he asked as she drank water.

"I am drinking water. What are you doing?"

He moved to the door. "I am opening the door. What are you doing?"

"I am putting wood on the fire. What are you doing?"

"I am looking at your seashells. What are you doing?" he asked, with such a peculiar expression on his face that she laughed.

"I am jumping up and down. What are you doing?"

"I am walking to you."

"Toward you."

"I am walking toward you. What are you doing?"

"I'm still jumping. What are you doing?"

"I am walking closer toward you."

"To you."

"To you. And closer. What are you doing?"

She stopped jumping. "I am standing still," she said. "I am walking. Closer. Closer."

She stood very still, silent, watching him come, the sea-dragon in the prince's body, with the gold in his hair and the firelight sliding over his skin. "I am coming very close."

She swallowed. "Very close."

"I am touching you." His hands were on her shoulders. Then she saw the simple need in his eyes, and she put her arms around him.

"I am touching you."

"Yes," he said softly, and she felt the long sigh through his body. "You are touching me."

She watched him fall asleep in front of the fire. Her heart ached at his loneliness. Like Kir, he was bound to the sea, in body if not in heart, and loving him was no more possible than loving his brother, whose wild heart cried out to follow the tide.

"Lyo," she whispered, "what are we going to do?" But there was no answer from the sleeping magician.

Eight

Then the sea, missing its gold, perhaps, began to play tricks on the fishers. Enin told the first tale, coming in late on a spring evening with Tull Olney dragging behind him. Enin was soaking wet, his face pale, his eyes bloodshot from salt water. He stood at the bar, dripping on the floor, downing beer as if to wash salt out of his throat. Tull, as bedraggled as Enin, looked, Mare said later, as if he had been slapped silly by a dead cod. Peri, coming up from the kitchens with a warm loaf of bread wrapped in her skirt, stopped short on the top of the stairs when Tull said, "There is something going on in the sea."

"There's something going on in your head," Enin said brusquely. "I'll have another beer."

"You heard the singing!"

"I heard somebody blowing a conch. That's all." He turned to the fishers and the innkeeper, and Mare, who had slipped in at the sound of his voice. "Tull and I were fishing close by each other. He says he heard singing, I say a conch shell. It was near sundown, the sea was milky-blue under a sweet south wind. I heard a conch—"

"Singing," Tull muttered into his beer.

"It was that deep, foggy sound. A conch, like they use up in the north villages to call all the fishers together. I heard a splash, and there was Tull, leaping out of his boat to swim with his boots on after a seal!"

"It wasn't a seal!"

"I called out to him, he never answered, just swam on. Then the seal dove under, and Tull was left floundering in the water with his fishing boots filling up. So guess who got to leap in after him?" He downed half his second glass and glared at Tull. Peri, watching him with her mouth open, saw something frightened behind the glower. Tull banged his own glass onto the bar.

"It was singing! And it was a woman!"

"It was a seal! A white seal—"

"It was a white-haired woman, with—"

"With brown eyes."

"With brown eyes." Tull looked around the silent room, his own eyes round, stunned. "She sang. She was a small, pretty thing, white as shell, playing in the water as if she had been born in it. She flicked water at me, laughing, and then . . . there I was. Like Enin said. Jumping into the deep sea as careless as if I were a seal myself." He shuddered. "She vanished, left me hanging there in the empty ocean. Her singing . . . it was like singing out of a dream I wanted to find my way into. I started trying to drink the sea, then, and Enin pulled me out."

The fishers stared at him, lamplight washing over

their still faces. Somebody snickered. Ami dropped her face in her arms, whimpering with laughter.

"A seal. You prawn-eyed loon, leaping into the deep sea to frolic with a seal!"

"It wasn't a seal!"

"Next it'll be the King of the Sea himself blowing his conch in your ear."

"I almost drowned," Tull said indignantly, but by then everyone was laughing too hard to listen to him.

Peri, hugging the warm loaf to her for comfort, left quickly, passing Mare in the doorway, staring at Enin and Tull without a glimmer of a smile on her face.

Next, it was Bel and Ami who came in late, quarreling bitterly over a lost net. Something, it transpired, had come up in their haul that Ami refused to pull in.

"It was an old dead hammerhead," Bel said disgustedly.

"It was a boy!" Ami wailed. "A luminous, shiny green-white mer-boy, caught in the net among all the fish. I thought he was dead, but he opened his eyes and smiled at me."

"She let go of the net. It was so heavy I couldn't hold it," Bel said. "Heavy as if someone were beneath, pulling it down. Ami was screeching in my face. I had to let go finally to shake her. A mer-boy, my left ear. It was nothing but a dead shark. Now we need a new net."

In the next week or so, half the fishers hauled in a tale along with their day's catch, and nobody was laughing anymore. One fisher had nearly rammed his boat against rocks, trying to join a pair of lovely sirens drying their long hair in the sun. Another, beckoned by a vague figure in a strange boat toward a wondrous school of fish, rowed dangerously far out to sea, only to watch the strange boat flounder and sink, as it had many years before. There were tales of hoary, tentacled, kelp-bedecked sea monsters, and of great ghostly ships from some forgotten past rising silently out of the water to sail right through the fishing boats like some icy, briny fog. The fishers' catch dwindled; the innkeeper had trouble keeping beer in stock. Worse, the summer visitors had caught wind of the tales and were passing them gleefully along to one another.

"We'll be the laughing stock of the island," Enin said glumly, leaning on a doorpost and watching the girls work. "Soon we'll be too frightened to stick our bare feet in the surf, let alone leave the harbor."

"They want their gold back," Mare said soberly.

"We haven't got it!"

"I know."

"That chowderhead mage turned it into flowers."

"I know."

"Well, what are we supposed to do?"

Mare stopped shoveling ashes out of the hearth. "I think you'd better find that magician before whatever is in the sea drives you onto land for good. But," she added, shoveling furiously again, "since you never paid any attention to me before—"

"Now, Mare," Enin said, coughing at the cloud she raised.

"It's not likely any of you will have enough sense to now."

"Where would he have got to, do you think?"

"You found him before, you can find him again."

Enin sighed. "We'll be a laughingstock."

"So? Who in this village is laughing anymore?"

Was it the gold, Peri wondered as she walked back that evening? Or was it the king's son the sea wanted back, chained again, not knowing any human language? He would come that night; he came every night. She was getting used to waking in the dark to his gentle voice saying unexpected things. She felt a chill down her back, though the air was balmy. The sea was troubling the fishers now. How long would it be before it found its way to her door? Lyo had freed the sea-dragon from the gold chain, but not from the sea. He could not live on land any more than his half-brother could live in water. Who could help them? Where was Lyo? Where were any answers for either of them? She stopped mid-step in the sand, feeling too helpless and worried to think any longer; she could only shout hopelessly as loud as she could, in frustration, expecting no answer.

"Lyo!"

"What?" he said beside her. Her shout turned into a scream; she seemed to levitate before his eyes. He bent quickly to pick up the mussels she had dropped. She came back down to earth finally and glared at his shaking shoulders.

"Lyo, where have you been?"

"Here." His voice sounded constrained; he had to duck away from her again, while a sound like geese arguing came out of him.

"Well, why didn't you tell me?"

"Why didn't you call me before?"

"How should I know you would come?"

"I'm sorry—" He straightened finally, wiping his eyes. "You looked so—all your hair went straight for a moment, like a giant hedgehog. I've never seen anything like it."

"It did not." But she was smiling then, too, at the sound of his cheerful voice and at his secret, dancing eyes. She held out her skirt; he dropped the mussels back into it.

"Lyo, something is happening in the sea," she said.

"I know. I've been hearing the tales."

"Have you seen anything, when you're with the sea-dragon?"

"No."

"It's the sea-dragon the sea wants back."

"Do you think so?"

"What else could have upset it? The fishers think it's happening because they tried to steal the gold."

"So." His mouth curled up at one corner. "Now they want me to put the chain back on."

"But if you do that—"

"I'm not going to."

"But if you don't, the fishers will be frightened out of the sea. They have to make a living."

"I know."

"Then what will you do?"

He tugged his hair into spikes, smiling at her again. Then his eyes strayed to the sea idling between the spires. "Well. We know that paths exist between land and sea. Kir's mother found one. I have spent some time searching for a way for humans to reach that country beneath the sea."

"Walk there?" she breathed, appalled and fascinated at the same time.

"People do. Sometimes. But not easily, and sometimes at an extraordinary price. Time passes differently in the undersea; humans can lose years, memories, loves, other things they value. Getting back is even more difficult."

"Oh." She sighed slowly. "Then what—"

"The only thing I can think of that might help is to talk to Kir's mother."

Peri looked at him out of the corners of her eyes. "His mother."

"She stole the king's human son, she chained him, she bore the king's sea-child. Maybe she is responsible for the things happening to the fishers. Maybe she is trying to speak to the king that way, sending him a message, making him pay attention to the sea."

"Except that he's not here."

"But we are. We're listening."

"Would she want to talk to you?"

"Us."

"You. She has never even talked to Kir."

"Sometimes people get so angry they can't hear anything beyond their anger."

"Who is she angry at?"

"The king."

"Still? After all these years?"

"I suppose she still loves him."

"How can she love him and be so angry with him at the same time?" Peri asked, bewilderedly.

"It happens often," Lyo said. He stopped to pick up an agate in his lean, quick fingers and look through it at the sun. "Love and anger are like land and sea: They meet at many different places. The king has two sons. One he knows, the other he doesn't. It's about time he met his wife's true child."

"But he only looks human for a couple of hours every night. The rest of the time he looks like a sea-dragon.

You can't row the king out to sea and introduce him to a sea-dragon.''

"No.''

"Well, then—'' Her voice faltered. "Well, then, how can you—Lyo, no.''

"It's the only way.''

"No.'' She gripped his arm, pleading. "No. Please, no. You can't bring the king to my house.''

"Peri, he has to know that he has another son. And if we don't do something soon, the fishers will be driven entirely out of the sea. Or else the sea-dragon will be chained again, so deeply that he will be lost forever. Were you thinking you could just teach him enough language so that he could find his own way to his father's house?''

Peri shook her head. "I don't know,'' she said numbly. "I wasn't thinking. But who knows when Kir and the king will be back?''

"Kir still doesn't know he has a brother?''

"He left just before the sea-dragon changed. He never guessed that part of the story.''

Lyo grunted, thinking. "You tell him when he returns. I'll tell the king.''

Peri stared at him. "You aren't afraid? You'll walk into his house and tell him he has a secret son in the shape of a sea-dragon living in the sea?''

Lyo shrugged imperturbably. "Someone has to. Three people know: you, me, and Kir's mother. That leaves me.''

The next day and the next brought in more tales from the sea: of something coming alive in a net, wrapping caressing arms around a fisherman's neck and nearly pulling him under the water; of a strange cloud that swallowed two or three boats on a cloudless day. Fog-blind, lost, they drifted aimlessly for hours, hearing bells ring, occasional laughter, sometimes a sweet, astonishing harping, faint and light as a sudden patter of rain beyond the cloud. The boats came out of the cloud near nightfall, without a fish in their holds, and so far from the harbor it took them until midnight to get back. All the fishers were looking haunted; they sent messages traveling up and down the coast, pleading for the return of the magician.

"It's all the old stories out of the sea coming alive," Mare said wonderingly, as they put mops and brushes and dust cloths away at the end of the day. "I wonder who it was we offended, making all that gold disappear."

"And we never got so much as a coin out of it," Carey sighed. "It's not fair. The magician probably stole it. He probably picked all the flowers out of the water and turned them into gold again. He won't come back."

"Ah, don't say that. He's our only hope."

"Maybe. Maybe the king can do something when he comes back."

"What could he do? Even if he believed the fishers? I can't see him jumping out of his great ship with his boots on to swim after a seal. He watches the waves from his fine house; he sails from land to land on his ship; the only fish he sees are covered with sauce on his plate. What does he know about the sea?"

"Something," Peri muttered without thinking.

"What?"

She tugged at her hair until it fell over her eyes. "I said something. Maybe that's what he can do. Maybe."

There was a storm that night. Dark, swollen clouds gathered at the horizon at sunset, moved inland fast. Peri heard rain thump on the roof as she cooked supper. In the middle of the night, she woke to the crash of thunder, and she got up to watch the sea-dragon tumble in on the wild waves. The sea washed him out more quickly than usual; he was drenched with rain by the time he reached Peri's door.

She threw blankets over him; he stood in front of the fire, his teeth chattering. Then, as he drank the hot broth she gave him, gradually he began to speak. The storm had not upset him, she realized; to him it was just another form of water.

"I saw a boat," he said.

"A boat?" she repeated, horrified. "A fishing boat? In that storm?"

He shook his head, flicked water out of his bright hair with one hand. "Not boat. The word is too small. Bigger than a boat. After the sun went down. Far away. I swam so far the land was thin."

"A ship!"

"A ship," he agreed. "In the rain. I swam with it listening to the voices."

"It's a rough night for a ship to be out," Peri said. She was frowning, her arms folded tightly, protectively; she was nervous at what she wanted to say to him. He put his hand to her face suddenly, where her brows were trying to meet.

"What are you doing?"

"What? Oh—" Her brows jumped apart again. "I was frowning. That's a frown."

He tried it, his hand still touching her face. Then he

laughed. He said, watching her closely when she didn't laugh, "Your face is talking. I can't hear it."

She held herself more tightly, drew a breath. "When you—when you swim in the sea, do you have a name?"

He was very still then; his hand dropped. His eyes left her face, went to the fire. He drew the blankets more closely about him. When she realized he would not, or could not, answer, she tried again.

"Who put the chain around you?"

Still he didn't answer. He kept his eyes on the fire, as if he were listening to its voice. She said softly, her brows puckered worriedly, "This is the world you belong in. Not the sea. You belong here, in this world of air and fire; you were born to walk on this land. All the worlds above the sea belong to you. Tell me. If you can. If you remember. Who chained you to the sea?"

He looked at her finally. Fire-streaked tears ran down his face; he made no sound. She swallowed, reaching out to him, touching him. He lifted one hand after a moment, brushed it across his cheek and stared down at it.

"What am I doing?"

"Crying," she whispered. "You are crying tears. Sea-children don't cry."

"Tears."

"You are sad." She put her hand on her heart. "Here. What made you cry?"

He looked down at the fire again, seeing in its drifting, eddying flames a land she could not imagine. "I don't have the words," he said softly. "You teach me."

"What—what words do you need?"

"All the words," he said, "under the sea."

Perplexed, she stopped on the beach the next evening

and summoned the magician from whatever secret place he kept himself. She had caught him in the middle of a bite; he offered her a piece of his bread and cheese while he finished chewing.

"Lyo," she said, her mouth full.

"Yes."

"Where are you when you're not here?"

"Oh." He swallowed, waved a hand inland. "There's a bit of forest beyond the gorse. . . . What is it?"

"I need something."

"What do you need?"

"Something with words in it."

"A book?" he suggested. She frowned at him dubiously. He asked delicately, trying not to smile, "Can you read?"

"Of course I can read," she said witheringly. "Everyone can. It's just that after you learn how, it's not something you do."

"Oh."

"Not in this village, anyway. My mother has a book she presses flowers in. But it's not what I need."

"What—"

"I need something for the sea-dragon. Lyo, my house is too small; there are no more words in it. He wants to tell me something about the land under the sea, but he doesn't know the words, and I can't teach him, because I don't know what he's seeing."

"Ah," Lyo said, illuminated. Then his thoughts went away from her; his eyes grew blue-black, absent. "But," he said, coming back, "you must be careful."

"Of what?"

"Of the book."

"What book?"

"Tut," he said. "Pay attention, Periwinkle. The spell book. Don't read it, just look at the pictures. They should help you. Promise you won't try to work the spells."

"I promise," she said, bewildered but entranced.

"I'm very serious. You'll make all your hair fall out, you'll turn yourself into something."

"A periwinkle?"

He laughed, then, forgetting his warnings. "Perhaps."

"Lyo. Did you turn that gold into periwinkles on purpose?"

His eyes grew light, dancing, making her smile. "Well. Your name was on my mind."

"Did you?"

"What a dull place the world would be if all the mysteries in it were solved. Wait here." He vanished, leaving, Peri's bemused eyes told her, his shadow on the sand. He was back in a moment, chewing again, with a huge black book under one arm. *"Elementary Dealings with the Sea,"* he said, passing it to her; their hands seemed to blur a little into its darkness. Then Lyo murmured something, and the hazy lines of the book firmed. "It's open, now. It's a sort of primer for beginning mages."

"Oh."

"Don't worry," he said reassuringly, "it has lots of pictures." He paused, his voice on the edge of saying something more. Then he nudged at an expired jellyfish with his foot. "Call me again when you need me."

"How can you hear me out there in the forest?"

"It's easy. Your voice comes out of nowhere, catches me like a fishhook in my collar, and hauls me to where you are.'' She laughed, feeling a sudden color running up under her cheeks. He smiled his quick, slanting smile, then sobered. ''Be careful,'' he said again; she nodded absently.

The book had wondrous pictures. She lay beside the hearth that evening, turning pages slowly and dropping crumbs between them as she nibbled her supper. Pictures accompanied each mysterious spell. At first glance they were simply paintings, but as she gazed at them longer, they began to move. Whitecaps swelled; wind picked up spindrift, flung it like rain across the surface of the sea: ''How to Achieve a Minor Storm.'' Mermaids swam among languorous kelp forests: ''How to Attract the Attention of Certain Inhabitants of the Sea.'' Between a glass-still sea and hot, windless blue sky, a ship's sails began to billow: ''How to Inspire Breezes in a Dead Calm.'' A dark, beautiful horse rode out of the surf: ''Recognizing Certain Dangerous Aspects of the Sea.'' Kir, she thought, recognizing him. The dark rider out of the sea . . . She fell asleep with her face against the dark horse and woke hours later, stiff and cramped beside the cold hearth, with the puzzled sea-dragon kneeling beside her, asking, ''What are you doing?''

She built a fire quickly, showed him the pictures shifting under the trembling light. ''Look,'' she said. ''Lyo's book.''

''Book.''

''These are pictures. These are words.'' He looked dubiously at the faded writing on the pages, but the pictures fascinated him. Fish and sea-beasts swam through its pages. Sometimes he gave a chuckle of recognition and pointed for her to tell him a word.

"Sea-cow. Porpoise. Whale."

She turned a page that seemed nothing more, at first, than a painting of the bottom of the sea, full of giant kelp and coral colonies and clams and brightly colored snails strewn thickly across sand. Then the picture changed, as if water had rolled over it, altered it to reveal, behind the kelp, faint, luminous towers of shell and pearl. The sand turned into paths of pearl, the bright shells to gold and jewels scattered along the paths as if they might have fallen a long way from great ships wrecked and sunken and snagged by underwater cliffs on their cold journey down. Peri, her lips parted, peered closer. Was there a figure walking down a path? A woman, perhaps, clothed in pearl, her long hair drifting behind her, adorned with tiny starfish and sea anemones?

The sea-dragon made a sound. His face was very white; his open hand fell across the page as if to block it from his sight.

"Chain," he whispered. He looked at Peri, struggling to talk; the words were still trapped, in spite of everything Peri had done, behind his eyes. "Here." The woman took a slow step; the water shifted again, hid the magic kingdom. But the sea-dragon saw it, hidden within the dark kelp. "Here. It began."

Nine

The next morning, Peri found a black pearl on her doorstep.

Her shriek startled Lyo out of his secret forest, brushing leaves out of his hair, his eyes so dark they looked black as the pearl. He took it from her silently, gazed at it as she babbled. It was the size of an acorn, perfectly round, with a sheen on it like dusky silk. He whistled.

"It's very beautiful."

"Lyo!"

"Well, imagine what great oyster fretted itself unknowingly, growing this in silence out of a grain of sand." He tossed it absently into the air, caught it, his eyes narrowed at the bright morning sea.

"Lyo, an oyster didn't roll across the sea and bring me this! She knows this is where the sea-dragon comes! She'll find him here, she'll chain him again—"

"No, she won't."

"But—"

"She sent you a message."

"Yes!"

"She said 'I know about you, you know about me.' If she wanted the sea-dragon back, she would take him, she wouldn't bother putting pearls on your doorstep. She permits the sea-dragon to come here. Although," he added, veering off into his own thoughts, "why for only a couple of hours in the dead of night is a mystery. Nothing about any of this makes much sense. The magic seems so confused. . . ."

"Well, what does she want?" Peri demanded, confused herself. "Lyo, what does she want? The sea-dragon recognized her last night—or someone like her. She walked through one of the paintings in your book. Someone saw her to be able to paint her like that, someone went down to the undersea, and came back up. So why can't Kir do it? Why can't you? Go down and ask her what she wants?"

"Have you ever seen a mermaid?"

"No."

"But you could draw one?"

"Yes."

"How? If you've never seen one?"

"I don't know. Everyone knows what a mermaid looks like. Now," she sighed, "they're even seeing them."

"But they knew the word before they saw the mermaid."

She nodded, perplexed. "People tell stories," she said finally.

"And words," Lyo said, "like treasures, get handed down through time. Very, very few people make a real journey to the undersea. It is a journey out of the world. But everyone who tells the tale of a sea-journey, or listens to it, travels there safely and comes back again. So don't assume the painter went down to view that world firsthand. Perhaps he painted his own sea-journey that he made through his mind when he first heard the tale.''

"Yes, but," Peri said, "Lyo, the sea-dragon recognized her."

Lyo grunted. His fingers searched his hair, picked out a bit of twig. "Well," he admitted, "maybe you're right. Long ago, the painter went down and came back, bearing a sea-treasure of strange knowledge. . . . But neither you nor I are going to do that."

"Then how will you talk to Kir's mother?"

"We. We are going to do a little fishing with the fishers."

"Most of the fishers don't go out now," she said. "They say there's a storm at sea, and they'll wait it out like any other storm."

"Has anyone gotten hurt?"

"No. But—"

"Then let's go. Unless you'd rather wait and see what you find on your doorstep tomorrow morning."

"No," she whispered. "I wouldn't."

The few fishers braving the sea's tantrum had left the harbor by the time they reached the docks; no one saw the magician everyone was searching for except a half-dozen gulls sunning on the posts. Lyo charmed a few barnacles off the underside of the *Sea Urchin* as he dipped oars into the water. This time, Peri knew, he used magic to row; they cleared the harbor and were into open sea faster than was decent for a small fishing boat. But instead of joining the vague dots on the horizon, he pursued his own course, rowing parallel to the land, heading toward the deep waters beyond the spires.

Peri, damp and numb, watched the tall rocks inch closer. She had never seen them from that angle. She had looked between them out to sea, but she had never seen them frame the land as if they were some giant broken doorway between the sea and the land. As Lyo rowed closer, the landscape between the spires changed: now empty, bright sea, now a wave tearing at a crumbling cliff, now white sand and a green wall of gorse, now the old woman's house between them, looking tiny and faded between the great, dark, sea-scoured stones, the way it might look to a sea-dragon or to someone swimming between them, carrying a black pearl like a message from the sea. . . . She blinked. Were the spires a doorway to the land or to the sea? Who was looking out? Who looked in? Which was the true country?

Then, as she blinked again, a cloud fell over them, pearl white, chill, blinding. Lyo stopped rowing. They stared at one another, their hair beaded with mist. The sea, reflecting a cloudless sky moments before, had turned a satiny gray. Peri heard a light laugh, almost a sound water might have made lapping against the underside of a boat, but not quite. She slid to the floor of the boat, holding herself tightly, trembling with cold. Something shook the *Sea Urchin*'s bow, a giant hand beneath the water playing with a toy boat. Peri tried to make herself smaller. Lyo, his face oddly milky in the strange mist, stood up and tossed the black pearl back into the sea.

A hand reached out of the water and caught it. A face looked up at them from beneath the cold, gentle water.

Long hair coiled and uncoiled. Starfish clung to it, and sea-flowers, and long, long loops of many-colored pearls. The face was very pale; the heavy, almond-shaped eyes held all the darkest shades of mother-of-pearl . . . Kir's eyes.

She was very close to them, yet farther than a dream, just beneath the waves sliding softly over her face. She held the pearl underwater in her open palm, waiting, it seemed to Peri, for something to happen. Nothing did. Lyo looked transfixed by her. She watched them, swaying beneath the water, her eyes expressionless, or too strange to read. She said something finally; bubbles flowed upward. The words themselves, popping out of the water, sounded very distant. Lyo smiled. He picked periwinkles out of the mist and scattered them on the water. A few drifted down, clung to her hair. She smiled, then, a small, careful smile without much humor in it.

"What did she say?"

"She said," Lyo answered, "that I am very strong."

"That's a peculiar thing to say," Peri said morosely.

"Not really." His voice shook; she realized then that some of the mist beading his face was sweat. "We're having an argument at the moment about who is going to do what to the *Sea Urchin's* bow."

Peri closed her eyes. "I wish I were at work," she whispered. "I wish I were scrubbing floors, I wish I were—"

"Where's your sense of adventure?"

"I never had one. What happens if you lose?"

"I don't think I'd better."

A sudden thought cleared Peri's head. She opened her eyes, stared at the little pool of water that had splashed into the bottom of the boat. She was still shivering with cold, but her fear had gone. "Ask her," she said tightly, "if she tried to wreck this boat before. Ask her if she recognizes it."

Lyo rolled his eyes at her. A sea gull with blood-red eyes had come out of nowhere to sit on his shoulder. "You ask her," he said.

Peri leaned against the side of the boat, stared down at the woman with Kir's eyes who floated as easily as moonlight on the water. "Did you?" she whispered; in that close, strange mist it seemed even a tear falling into the water would echo. "Did you take my father out of this boat when he went out to fish? My mother thinks you did. She looks for the land beneath the sea. She thinks he's there now, that you took him there and sent his boat back to us empty."

The woman gazed back at her, her eyes secret, unblinking. She spoke again; her voice sounded like water trickling in some hidden place.

Peri looked at Lyo. "What did she say?"

"She said that no one from the world of air has come into the sea-kingdom for many years." The sea gull was nibbling at his ear; he shrugged a shoulder irritably and it flew off with a cackle.

"He went out to sea," Peri said, "and never came back."

"Many fishers do that," Lyo said gently. "They take such risks." The woman said something else, her hand closing and opening again on the pearl. Peri, listening closely, could not unravel her words from the murmur of the tide.

"If your father had cast his heart into the sea, his body might have wandered into her country," Lyo translated. "But his heart came with his boat into harbor every night. So his bones may be in this sea, but his heart remains where he kept it all his life."

Peri was silent. The woman, silent, too, studied her. The *Sea Urchin*'s bow had not wavered from pointing at the same distant tangle of gorse; she still held it. Her face blurred slightly under a wash of foam; long, pale hair drifted. She spoke again.

"She says she has no quarrel with the fishers."

"Not for wanting her gold?"

"She says the gold falls out of the lost ships into her country like rain falls on land. It means little to her; it is the work of men, and belongs to the country above the waves."

"Then what does she want?"

The woman's other hand rose out of the water; she tossed something silver into the boat. It struck the wood at Peri's feet, and she jumped. Lyo picked it up.

"A ring," he said. His voice shook again, strained. "Letters on it—"

"*U,V,*" Peri breathed. "It's the king's ring. I threw it into the sea."

"Of course. I should have guessed. Young floor-scrubbers are constantly throwing kings' rings into the sea."

"Kir brought it to me." Her eyes widened then, she added urgently, "Lyo, tell her about Kir—"

"She knows about Kir. She gave him to the king. What do you think this tempest is all about?"

"But, tell her—" She gripped the side of the boat and leaned far over, until it should have tilted, and said it herself. "Kir! Kir wants to come to you! Please let him in! Please—"

"Peri!" Lyo shouted. Pale hands came up out of the water, caught Peri's wrists, and pulled her down until the *Sea Urchin* was almost on its side. Peri's own hair floated in the water; the sea washed over her face and she sputtered. The water was icy. She drew a breath to scream, and drew in another swell instead. Then the *Sea Urchin* lurched; she tumbled down to the bottom of the boat, spitting out sea water, her eyes and nose running. The bow was free, drifting; the fog seemed to be thinning. Lyo was staring at her hands.

"What are you holding?"

She blinked salt water out of her eyes. Webs of pure moonlight attached to irregular circles and squares of twigs and dried seaweed . . . She sniffed, wiped her nose on her sleeve, still blinking. In the center of each web was a tiny crystal-white moon. She caught her breath.

"My hexes!"

"Your what?"

"My hexes. I made them to hex the sea. Lyo, look at them!"

"I am," Lyo said wonderingly.

"She turned my black thread into moonlight!"

"Wait—"

"I made them without moons and threw them into the sea with the king's ring. I thought the sea-dragon ate them!"

The fog had blown away; they were wallowing perilously close to the spires. Lyo plied the oars, fighting the tide. Gulls cried, circling the spires; a sea otter, on its back in the waves, cracking a shell against the stone on its belly, paused to give them a curious look.

"I think," Lyo said, with a neighborly nod at the sea otter, "you'd better begin at the beginning. Begin with the word hex. Who taught you to make one in that shape?''

''The old woman.''

''What old woman?''

''The old woman who disappeared, whose house I've been staying in, she taught me. I made hexes to throw into the sea because it took my father—that's when I first saw the sea-dragon.''

''When—''

''When I threw the hexes in. Kir was looking for the old woman, too, and he found me on the cliff drawing hexes in the sand.''

Lyo pulled the oars up, leaned on them, looking at her. The *Sea Urchin* continued along its course. ''Kir knew the old woman, too?''

''He said she came out to watch the sea with him, once. He wanted to talk to her; he said she knew things. But she had already gone.''

''Gone where?''

''Just gone. She went away and never came back.'' She sighed a little, her eyes on the tiny house tucked into the gorse.

Lyo said gently, ''People left you, this past year.''

She nodded. ''My mother, too. She didn't leave— she— It's like you said. She went on a sea-journey, in her mind. She hasn't come back yet. Anyway, when Kir found me drawing hexes, he asked me to send the sea a message for him.''

''And the message was?''

''Part of it was his father's ring.''

The magician said, ''Ah,'' very softly. His arms were still propped on the oars; his eyes, for some reason, were gray as gulls' wings. "And now the sea has returned the king's ring and your hexes."

"But she changed my hexes. They were ugly before, twisted and dark—that's how I meant them to be. Now they're full of magic."

Lyo touched one lightly, curiously. "So they are," he murmured, and shook birds off the upended oars.

"But why? Why did she give them back?"

"Why is the wind, why is the sea . . . ? She gave them back for a very good reason."

"What reason?"

"I haven't the slightest idea," the magician said, and dipped the oars back into the water. Then his eyes fixed on something beyond Peri's shoulder, narrowed, and changed again. "Look."

She turned and saw the king's ship on the horizon, all its white and gold sails unfurled to the wind, wending its way back to the village.

Ten

Kir came with the night tide. Peri, sleeping restlessly, listening beneath her dreams for a wash of pearls across her threshold, woke slowly to the full, hollow boom of the breakers. The moon, three-quarters full, hung in her window, distorted, veined with crystal; it reminded her of the tiny, mysterious moons the sea-woman had woven into the hexes. It fashioned magical shapes out of the night: pearly driftwood and tangled seaweed, a prince mounted on a dark horse at the edge of the tide.

Peri, tide-drawn, pulled a quilt over her shoulders and opened her door. The moon eyed her curiously. She walked across the cool, silvery sand, the ebb and flow of tide singing in her head. As she neared the dark prince, his face turned away from the sea to her. He said nothing, simply held out his hand for her to mount. A wave foamed around her feet, coaxing; Kir pulled her up out of the water. He put his arms around her, his cheek against her hair. They sat silently, watching the water arch and break against the stones.

"I missed you," Kir said finally. He sounded surprised. "I thought of you in the North Isles."

"I thought of you," Peri whispered. She stopped to swallow. "Kir—"

"I saw the sea-dragon last night—was it last night? In a storm. It followed us for a long time."

"Kir, I have something to tell you."

"Then tell me."

"I saw your mother."

Kir said nothing; the words, she realized, must have made no sense to him at first. Then she felt the shock of them through his entire body. "What did you say?"

"Kir, strange things have been happening to the fishers, they see mermaids, hear singing, they get lost in sudden fogs—"

"Peri," Kir said tightly.

"That's what happened to us—"

"Who? What are you—"

"Lyo. The magician. He rowed us out there, beyond the spires, to look for your mother, to speak to her for you. A cloud came down over us on a cloudless morning. And your mother stopped our boat." A wave glimmered around them, pulled at the dark horse, melted away. "She had your eyes. And your father's ring."

He gripped her almost painfully. "It reached her—"

"She got your message. And she got mine. She gave me back my hexes." She could hear his breathing now, shaken, unsteady, and she twisted anxiously to face him, breaking his hold. "Lyo says she is angry at your father. She threw his ring into the boat. Lyo says she still loves your father."

"Lyo? The magician who turned the gold chain into flowers?"

"Periwinkles."

"Peri—" He stopped suddenly, his tongue stumbling on her name. "Periwinkles . . . I thought that was an inept thing to do. Until now. Did my mother—did she—"

"She sent a kind of message to you. I tried to ask her about you, and she nearly pulled me overboard, giving me the hexes. I don't understand it."

"I don't understand," he said raggedly, "why it was you who saw her and not me. I have been waiting so long."

"I know." She pulled his arms around her again, feeling a chill that only he could give or take away. "It should have been you. But Lyo said we had to go out—"

"Why?"

"Because she left a black pearl on my doorstep."

His voice rose. "Why your doorstep? Why you?"

She swallowed, holding his hands tightly in hers. "Kir, there's something else. But you have to wait."

"I have waited," he said, his voice dangerously thin.

"I mean, just a few minutes. Then you'll see why she left the message at my door. Please." She pushed closer to him, feeling the cold again. "Please."

"Is she coming here?"

"No. I can't make her come and go. Just . . . wait. A few minutes. Tell me what you did while you were away."

He was silent; she sensed, like a gathering tidal wave, his anger, frustration, bewilderment. The sea roared around them, tugging at Peri's trailing quilt. The dark horse stirred restively, protesting. The reins flicked up; Kir guided it out of the water.

"I met a lady in the North Isles." His voice sounded haunted, weary. "She was the daughter of a lord there. She was very pretty. Her hair was not a tangled mess, nor did she walk barefoot in the sand by moonlight." Peri eased against him, her eyes wide; his hand touched her hair, smoothed it away from his mouth.

"Nor," she whispered, "did she scrub floors."

"No. She was sweet tempered and intelligent. We talked together, rode together. Sometimes we danced. My father was pleased. At night, after everyone had gone to sleep, I went down the cliffs over which her father's house was built, and I stood on the rocks and let the tide break over me as if I were another rock. I waited for it to pull me in. But it never did."

"Kir . . ."

"Nor did she pull me into her world. I wished she could have. . . . And then we came home. From the day we left the North Isles until this moment I have not spoken to my father. I can't. If I did, I would tell him he must let me go. But I have no world to go to, no place. So I cannot leave him."

"Did she love you? The lady from the North Isles?"

"I don't know. Perhaps, if I had been different, I might be there now, still dancing, watching her face in the moonlight. . . ." He touched Peri's cheek, turned her face; she felt the brush of his cold mouth. She put her arms around him, held him tightly, her eyes closed against the sea, as if by not seeing it, she could protect him. His hands slid through her hair, pulling her closer; she tasted the bitter salt on his lips. Then he pulled back, murmuring; she opened her eyes reluctantly. His face was turned as always toward the sea.

"What is that?" he breathed.

A shape, huge, dark, bulky, was rising out of the waves.

"It's the sea-dragon." Her voice shook. She felt her heartbeat, and a sudden chill that came from within her. The looming dark shape pushed closer to them through the surf; Kir rode farther up onto the sand.

"What is it doing?"

"It's coming out."

He was silent. The sea-dragon's eyes reflected moonlight, like two great, pale beacons. Its streamers tumbled in the tide, ribbons of light. Peri heard Kir swallow. "Why?" he asked abruptly. "Why does it come out?"

She shook her head slightly, too nervous to answer. The sea-dragon pulled relentlessly through the tide, up the gentle slope of wet sand, until it had coaxed all its fins and streamers out of the grasping tide. It was so close to them that its eyes seemed level with the moon. Kir's horse whuffed nervously at it; Kir held it still.

Then the extra moons vanished from the sky. While their eyes still searched bewilderedly for them, a young man rose from his knees on the sand, asked curiously, "What are you doing?"

Peri gathered breath. "He comes out," she said unsteadily, "to learn words."

Kir was still as a stone behind her. Then he moved, and she felt the cold at her back, all around her. Kir dismounted; the sea-dragon watched him calmly. The moonlight picked up strands of his gold hair. As Kir grew closer, the sea-dragon's expression changed; his brows twitched together. "What are you doing?" he whispered. He shivered suddenly, feeling the cold in his human form. "You are coming closer to me." Then his face smoothed again, with a look of wonder such as Peri had never seen on it before. He pulled a word out of nowhere like a mage: "Kir."

Kir stopped. Peri saw him trembling. Their faces, in profile against the bright waves, mirrored one another. Kir's hands moved; he unclasped the cloak at his throat, settled it over the sea-dragon's shoulders.

"What are you doing?" the sea-dragon asked again, pleading, Peri realized, for the sound of Kir's voice, a human voice answering his in the silence.

Kir spoke finally, his voice shaking, "I am looking at my brother."

Peri closed her eyes. She felt hands tugging at her, and she slid off the horse, hid her face against Kir, weak with relief. "You're not angry."

"How long—how long—"

"Since the night you left. It—he—came out of the sea then. The chain was gone. I never had a chance to tell you."

"No." She felt him trembling. "I should have guessed. The chain—"

"Chain," the sea-dragon echoed. He hovered uncertainly at the tide's edge, watching them.

"What is his name?" Kir asked.

"I don't think anyone gave him a name. He can only stay out of the sea for a couple of hours in the night, then he must go back to the sea-dragon's shape."

"Does my father know?"

"Lyo is going to tell him."

He looked at her. "Lyo," he said flatly. "Lyo. Who

exactly is this magician who likes periwinkles, and who isn't afraid to tell my father something like this?"

"I don't know," she said nervously. "Come to the house. I'll make a fire."

Sitting at her hearth, the two princes, one fair, one dark, looked startlingly alike. They were both of the same build, the same height. The sea-dragon, with Kir's dark cloak clasped with a link of pearls at his throat, studied Kir out of eyes a lighter blue than his own. That and their expressions differed. The sea-dragon, who had endured years of rolling winter storms, and who had been unthreatened by them, thwarted by nothing but a chain, seemed much calmer. Kir's face changed like the changing face of fire.

Peri opened Lyo's book, showed Kir the shifting, misty sea-gardens, the woman walking slowly away from them down the glittering path until the currents swirled through the kelp and the painting changed. The sea-dragon made a sound; Kir's eyes went to him.

"You know this place."

"When—when I was small, the chain was small," the sea-dragon said carefully. "The chain grew bigger. But it always began here."

Kir looked at the page, his eyes hidden again, but Peri saw the hunger in his face.

"It's like moonlight," he whispered, as the picture changed again. "You can see it, but you cannot hold it; it makes a path across the sea, but you cannot walk on it. I could look all my life and die before I found this place, and he is trying to escape from it." The sea-dragon was listening to him intently, trying to comprehend. Kir's eyes strayed to the writing beside the picture; the sea-dragon slid his hand over the words.

"What do you see?" he asked.

"A world I want." His face eased a little at the sea-dragon's expression. "You don't understand."

"I understand your words," the sea-dragon said. "I don't understand—" He made a little, helpless gesture. "Your eyes. You watch the sea. Even with Peri, you watch the sea."

Kir was silent, perhaps seeing himself on the shore through the sea-dragon's eyes. "Yes," he said softly. "I watch. I want to go there." He tapped the sea-world with his finger. The sea-dragon looked pained.

"You must not. You—" He shook his head, bewildered. Then things seemed to swirl together in his head into a picture; his eyes widened as he saw it. "Once there was a king who had two sons, one by the queen, his wife, and one by a woman out of the sea. . . . You," he said to Kir abruptly. "You." He touched Kir's face gently, near his eyes. Then he touched the woman with the starfish in her hair, whose heavy, blue-black eyes he had looked into beneath the sea. "You are the son out of the sea."

"Yes," Kir whispered. "Yes."

"I am not."

"No. You are not."

The sea-dragon looked bewildered again. "Then why am I in the sea?"

Kir's eyes rose, met Peri's. "Things happened," he said finally. "I don't understand all of them, either. I only know that you belong here on land, I belong in the country beneath the sea, with the woman who walks down those paths of pearl."

The sea-dragon was silent. His eyes shifted away to the fire; he gazed into it until Peri tugged at his arm, made him turn. He looked troubled, a new expression, one more movement into his human body.

"Kir," he said, his eyes on his brother's face. He paused, struggling for words; then he reached out, grasped Kir's shoulder. "I can see you. I can talk with you. To you. I come—I have come out of the sea to you. Stay. Here with Peri. In this world where I can see you."

"I can't stay," Kir said. His face looked white, stiff; Peri, watching anxiously, saw in amazement that he was close to tears. He moved after a moment, gripped the sea-dragon's wrist. "You can see me," he said huskily. "Peri can see me. No one else in the world can see what I really am. But I cannot stay with you here. I will die if I do not find my way into the sea."

"Die."

"Not live. Not see."

The sea-dragon loosed him reluctantly. "How?" he said, asking so many questions at once, it seemed, that Kir smiled.

"I don't know how," he said. "Perhaps the magician will find me a path. He seems adept at finding things." The sea shifted under his fingers then; he looked down at Lyo's book as if he had felt the changing. "There are ways," he said slowly, "written in here."

"Lyo said not to—"

"Lyo does not need to get into the sea."

"No," Peri said patiently, "but he said the spells are dangerous."

"Do you think I care?" he asked her patiently, and she felt her hands grow cold.

"You are not a mage."

"I can read," he said inarguably, and did so, while

the sea-dragon watched wonderingly and Peri got up and rattled pots and spoons, trying to distract Kir. She gave up finally, came to lean over his shoulder to see what he was reading.

"To find the path to the Undersea, find first the path of your desire," the spell book said mysteriously, next to a picture of a young woman standing in the surf, looking out to sea. Her hair was long, windblown; her feet were bare; a tear slid down her despairing face. Peri stared. Would she look like that when Kir finally left her? Her eyes went back to the script; her lips moved; she tried to memorize the spell in case she needed it.

"Call or be called," the spell said. Then: "Many paths go seaward. The path of the tide, the seal's path, the path of moonlight. The spiraled path of the nautilus shell may be imitated. Call or be called, be answered or answer. For those so called, this will be clear to their eyes. For others: You of a certain knowledge, a certain power, who wish for disinterested purposes to descend to the Undersea and return, it is imperative that a gift be taken. The gift must be of the value—or seem of the value—of the traveler's life. It may become necessary to make the exchange in order to return to time."

"I don't want to return," Kir murmured, frustrated.

"Wait," Peri said, fascinated. " 'Possessing the gift, the traveler must then find the path of the full moon at full tide, at the point where the path of the moon meets land.' It's not a full moon."

"It's almost full."

" 'There the traveler must reveal the gift to the sea and request, in fair and courteous voice, entry. Entry may be given by a dark horse appearing out of the foam, which the traveler will mount, a white seal, which the traveler will follow, by the sea queen herself, who will lead the traveler by moonlight to the country beneath the waves. The gift must be given at the time most appropriate for safe return. The journey is hazardous, not recommended unless all other courses are exhausted.' ''

"A gift," Kir said heavily.

"You gave her a gift: your father's ring."

"It wasn't worth my life. And she gave it back."

"You tried to give her your life once, too," Peri said. Her eyes filled with sudden tears at the memory, at his hopelessness. He stared into the fire, his face sea-pale, bitter.

"Perhaps," he said, "she does not want me."

"I think she does. Lyo thinks—"

"How would you know?" he demanded. "How would either of you know?"

The sea-dragon, startled at his raised voice, said softly, "What are you doing?"

Kir's mouth clamped shut. Peri turned away, ruffling at her hair, wondering suddenly if she understood anything at all of Kir's mother, of the strange world she dwelled in. The hexes on the spellbinding shelf caught her eye. She grabbed them desperately, scattered them across the spell Kir was reading.

"Look. Your mother gave me these when I said your name. They must mean something. They must!"

Kir stared at the webs of pearl and crystal and moonlight strung on odd bits of bent kelp. He held one up; fire beaded on it like dew. The round crystal in the center glowed like the sea-dragon's eye. He breathed, "What are they?"

"My hexes."

"They're beautiful. How did you—"

"She did it. I made them with black thread, your mother put the magic into them—" Her voice faltered. "Oh, Kir, look!" All around them on the walls and ceiling, the reflection of the hex Kir held trembled like a great, shining web of fire.

The sea-dragon made a sound, entranced. Kir turned the hex slowly; the web revolved around them. His lips moved soundlessly. He lifted his other hand, traced a thread; the shadow of his fingers followed the fiery pattern on the wall.

"But what?" he whispered. "But how?"

There was a knock at the door. They stared at it, preoccupied, uncomprehending, as if it were a knock from another world. The door opened. The king walked into the firelight, into the web.

Eleven ❧

He stopped short at the sight of the silent faces turned toward him, spangled with fire from the hexes. He had come plainly dressed; his long, dark, wool cloak hid darker clothes, but nothing could disguise his height, the familiar uplift of his head. He had given Kir his dark hair and his winging brows, even his expression; his gray eyes, unlike Kir's, were fully human. They moved from Kir to Peri, and then were caught by the sea-dragon. Fire and shadow shifted over the gold hair, the light blue eyes; the king closed his eyes, looking suddenly haunted.

Lyo stepped in behind him. He gazed in rapt abstraction at the tangle of fire on the walls. Then he saw the open spell book, and his eyes went to Peri, wide, questioning. Kir dropped the hex he held then, and the web vanished.

He got to his feet; so did the sea-dragon. Peri, huddled beside the hearth, wanted to rifle through the book for a vanishing spell. Kir and his father seemed at a loss for words.

The king said finally, "The mage told me you would be here. That this is where you come."

"Sometimes I come here," Kir said. He stopped to swallow drily. "Sometimes I just watch the sea."

The king nodded, silent again. His eyes moved in wonder and disbelief to the sea-dragon. Kir's hands clenched; Peri saw the sudden pain in his face.

"He is your son," Kir said abruptly. "Your true son. Take him and give me back to the sea."

The king was wordless, motionless for another moment. Then he reached Kir in two steps, his big hands closing on Kir's shoulders.

"You are my son." His hold rocked Kir slightly, then loosened a little. "You are so much like your mother," he continued huskily. "So much. I tried not to see it all these years. I didn't understand how it could be so. You have her eyes. I kept finding her face in my mind when I looked at you. Yet how it could be so . . . ?" His gaze shifted beyond Kir again to the sea-dragon. "And this one, this son, wearing the face of the young queen, the woman I married, and was only beginning to know when she died."

The sea-dragon moved to Kir's side, uneasy, Peri guessed, in the sudden, bewildering tension. The king's eyes moved, incredulous, from face to face, one dark, one fair, both reflections of a confused past.

"What are you doing?" the sea-dragon asked tentatively, startling the king.

Lyo said gently, "He doesn't know many words yet. Peri has been teaching him at night when he takes his human shape."

"Why only at night?" the king demanded. "Why does she still keep him in that shape? Is there a price I pay to take him from the sea? Is that it?"

Lyo, crossing the room to the spell book, knelt next to Peri. "I don't know," he said simply. "I think you should ask her."

The king's shoulders sagged wearily; he seemed suddenly dazed, helpless. He looked at Peri again where she crouched beside the fire, trying to hide behind Lyo, and she felt all her untidiness loom at once: her wild hair, her calloused hands, the patched quilt she had wrapped around her faded nightgown.

"You are my son's friend."

Peri's face flooded with color. She could stand up, then, as if the king's word gave her and her frayed quilt a sudden dignity. The sea-dragon curiously echoed the word, "Friend."

The king picked Peri's cloak off a chair and sat down tiredly. "The mage brought me a ring," he said. "My own ring. He told me who had thrown it into the sea. And who returned it from the sea." He studied Kir as he sat, as if, once again, he saw long pale hair braided with pearls floating on the tide. His voice gentled. "I thought you had fallen in love with some fisher's girl."

"I did," Kir said tautly.

"I thought that was what troubled you. I hoped it was only that. The mage said, if I wanted to do something wise for once, I should ask you what you want. He said—"

"How did you know?" Kir asked Lyo. His voice was very tense; the sea-dragon stirred, disquieted. Lyo looked up from the hexes scattered on the spell book.

He spoke calmly, but it seemed to Peri that he picked his words very carefully, as if he were devising a spell to avert a storm.

"Odd things draw my attention. Happiness, sorrow, they weave through the world like strangely colored threads that can be found in unexpected places. Even when they are hidden away, most secret, they leave signs, messages, because if something is not said in words, it will be said another way. In the city, I heard some fishers from a tiny coastal village wanting a great mage to remove a chain of gold from a sea-monster. Even before I saw the chain, I knew that the gold was the least important detail. What was important was the link someone had forged between water and air, between a mysterious place deep beneath the waves, and the place where humans dwell. And when I saw the sea-dragon, when I dipped behind its great eyes into its mind, I knew . . ."

"What did you know?" the king asked softly.

"Why it was drawn to the fishing boats, to every human voice. Why it rose above the waves to watch the land. And then I began to suspect why the king and his son came here so early this year, and why the prince was seen so often at odd hours of the day or night, riding that dark horse to the sea. . . . I didn't know then how much the king or the prince or the sea-dragon understood. I still don't know why it was finally permitted to be seen above the water. But I freed it, I turned the gold chain into flowers partly to disturb the sea, to send a message back to it. And partly because while gold will not float, periwinkles will. And then I tried to teach the sea-dragon a few things. It—he—found his own shape—I don't yet understand why or how. And he found Peri. Does he have a name?'' he asked the king, who shook his head. The king's face was very pale.

"I named my son after my wife died. My changeling child. Kir. I don't know if I ever saw my wife's true child. I named the child I saw Kir, and I remember thinking how dark his eyes were—a twilight dark—and thinking they would change into his mother's summer eyes. But they never changed.''

"And, in the sea, before she gave him to you, Kir's mother must have named him something. So Kir is twice-named—''

"Why would she have named me,'' Kir breathed, "to give me away? She must have hated us both—to chain him like that, to give me away—''

"She gave you to me,'' his father said sharply. "She knew I would love you. I loved her.''

Kir was silent, his hands opening, closing.

The king rose slowly, stood in front of him. "Is it so terrible?'' he asked painfully, "with me on land?''

"It is terrible,'' Kir said numbly. He lifted his face, so that the king could see his sea eyes. "I can't help it. I can't rest in this world. In the restless tide I can rest. I can't love in this world. Not even Peri.''

"You have loved me,'' she said, her voice shaking.

"No.''

"Yes. You have cared about me. You have thought of me.''

He gazed at her, mute again; his face changed with a flicker of light. He reached out, touched his father lightly, pleadingly. "Please. You must let me go.''

"How can you—'' The king stopped, began again. "How can you be so sure that when you are in the sea, you will not long just as passionately for this land?''

125

Firelight caught the glitter of unshed tears in his eyes. He swallowed, then added, the words coming with difficulty, "If you didn't want this so badly, I would never let you go."

"Please. Will you—will you talk to my mother?"

The king's eyes slipped away from him toward a memory. The harsh lines on his face eased, grew gentle, as if he might have been watching the soft blue sea on a summer's day. "Once," he whispered, "I could understand her strange underwater language."

The net of fire sprang around them once more. Lyo, toying with the hexes, had created such a tangle that they were cross-hatched with flaming threads. The seadragon murmured, "You are making the world into fire."

"It's not water, is it," Lyo said curiously. "Nothing that can exist in water . . . Strange, strange . . ."

"What are they?" the king asked. "Another message?"

"Yes. They're Peri's hexes. Kir's mother returned them like this, changed into moons and moon-paths, fire-paths."

"Why?"

"For us to use."

"How?"

Lyo shook his head, entranced, it seemed, by the weave of light. "I don't know," he whispered. "I don't know." Kir stood close to his father, watching. He seemed, Peri realized, finally becalmed; already he looked more like his mother, as if he were relinquishing his human experience. He found her looking at him wistfully; he gave her a sea-smile. She swallowed a

126

briny taste of sadness in her throat. Already he was leaving her.

The sea-dragon stirred restlessly: The tide called him, luring him out of his shape. "Peri," he said and she nodded. "I must go."

"What's to be done with him?" the king demanded of Lyo. The lines on his face deepened again. "Both my sons live in half-worlds. I will not lose them both to the sea."

The sea-dragon went to Kir, his fingers groping awkwardly at the clasp at his throat. Kir stopped him.

"Keep it," he said gently. "It's cold outside. I'll come with you to the tide's edge."

The sea-dragon shook his head. "No. Stay." They were all silent, hearing the tide as he listened to it. He smiled his untroubled smile, as if the rolling waves, the fish, and crying gulls were things he also loved, along with all the words he had learned, and Peri's human touch. Peri opened the door for him, put her arm around him in farewell. He started to take a step, then turned to look uncertainly at the king, as if struck by something—a web reflected around him—that he finally saw but barely understood.

"I want—" He struggled with the thought. "I must see you again."

The king's face eased with relief. "Oh, yes," he said. "Yes."

Peri left the top half of the door open, leaned out to watch the vague, moonlit figure cross the sand. Unexpectedly, Kir came to her. He slid his arms around her, leaned his face against her hair, watching over her shoulder. The king stood behind them both. The sea-dragon reached the tide's edge. He dropped Kir's cloak and walked naked into the sea, a pale, moonlit figure that gathered bulk and darkness as it changed.

A twig snapped in the utter silence; they all started. The king said explosively to Lyo, "Do something."

Lyo nodded, looking determined but a little blank. "Yes."

"You need a full moon," Peri said, remembering, and Lyo looked at her reproachfully. Kir's arms dropped; he turned restively.

"It wouldn't work for me."

"It should work," Lyo said. "Spells are in spell books because they work. Which is why—" He closed the book, sent it back, Peri supposed, to whatever bush he kept it under. Kir's eyes clung to him.

"A gift—it says I need—"

"Ah," Lyo said, shaking his head. "That's for mages. You have your heart's desire; that should be your path. You are the gift."

"But she didn't—she won't—"

"I know. I don't understand." He slid his fingers through his hair, left it standing in peaks. "The hexes. She gave the hexes to us so that we could use them. They are vital, they are necessary."

"How—"

"I don't know," he sighed. "Yet. We can only try."

"When?" the king asked.

"Five nights from now. When the moon is full. Meet me near the spires."

Kir nodded wordlessly. The king dropped a hand on his shoulder. "Come home for now," he said wearily, "while I still have a few days left of you. Your heart may be eating itself up to get into the sea, but I had you for seventeen years and when you leave me, you'll take what I treasured most. If the sea needs a gift, I'll give it.''

Kir's head bowed. He went to Peri wordlessly, kissed her cheek. Then he lifted her face in his hand, looked into her eyes. It won't be easy, his eyes said. It will not be easy to leave you.

''But I must,'' he said, and left her.

''The magician is back,'' Peri said absently, as she filled her bucket at the pump the next morning.

''Thank goodness,'' Mare breathed. ''The fishers will be able to work again.'' Carey leaped a little with excitement, slopping water.

''Will he get us the gold?''

''I don't know about the gold,'' Peri said. ''But I think he can stop the odd things happening in the sea.''

''But what about the gold?''

''He didn't say about the gold.''

''But why didn't—'' She stopped, her eyes narrowing on Peri's face. ''Why did he come to you? Where did you see him?''

Peri heaved her bucket aside to make room for Mare. ''He rowed out with me in the *Sea Urchin* yesterday. I think yesterday.'' It seemed suddenly a long time ago. She added to Mare, ''You can tell Enin that he's back.''

''I will.'' Mare's eyes narrowed, too, contemplating Peri as if she were beginning to see the misty, magical fog Peri moved in, where sea-dragons turned into princes at her feet, and kings knocked at her door. ''Why do I have the oddest idea that you know far more than you're saying about gold and mages and sea-dragons?''

Peri looked back at her mutely, clinging to her heavy

bucket with work-reddened hands. Her shoes and the hem of her dress were already wet. Mare shook her head slightly, blinking.

"No," she said. "Never mind. Silly thought." She pumped water into her bucket. Peri gazed at the bright morning sea. She swallowed a lump of sorrow, thinking of Kir, and of life without Kir, without the sea-dragon. An endless succession of scrub-buckets . . . For the first time, she understood Carey. A path of gold glittered away from the inn, leading to . . . what? It was the goldless floor-scrubber the two princes came to; no gold in the world could have bought her that: the magical kiss of the sea.

"Wake up," Mare said. Peri sighed and hefted her bucket.

Twelve

Five nights later, Peri sat at her window watching for the moon, waiting for Kir. Her face slid down onto her folded arms, she fell asleep and woke suddenly, hours later, drenched with light. A full moon hung above the spires; the breakers, slow and full, churned in its light to a milky silver before they broke.

She saw the rider beside the sea then, and her throat burned. Maybe, a tiny voice in her mind said, whatever Lyo does won't work, maybe he'll be forced to stay. . . . But even staying, he would always be someone found at the tide's edge, among the empty shells, looking seaward for his heart. Another horseman joined him: the king. They both looked seaward, down the dazzling path of light between the spires.

She opened her door, found Lyo on her doorstep. He, too, was watching the moonlight; his open hands were full of hexes.

He looked at her absently as she came out. "What do you think?" he asked. "One of them? All of them?"

"One of what?"

"The hexes."

"Are you going to hex the sea again?" she asked, confused, and he smiled.

"I hope not."

Her eyes went again to Kir; she sighed soundlessly, watching him, as he watched the sea. . . . Lyo was watching her. He gave her shoulder a quick, gentle pat.

"Come," he said, and she followed him across the sand. The beach between the house and the sea, between her and Kir, seemed to have stretched; the sand, strewn with driftwood and kelp, made her steps clumsy. She felt as she reached the bubbling, fanning tide, that she had traveled a long way to the dark rider, whose face was still turned away from her. Then he turned, was looking down at her; he slid off his horse and came to her.

He held her wordlessly; she blinked hot, unshed tears out of her eyes. He loosed her, held her hands, put something into them.

"What is it?" Her voice sounded ragged, heavy, as if she had been crying for a long time.

"It's the black pearl," he said softly, "that I will never dare bring you when I am in the sea." He kissed her cheek, her mouth; he gathered her hair into his hands. She lifted her face to meet his dark, moonstruck eyes.

"Be happy now," she whispered, aware of all the shining waves behind him reaching toward him, withdrawing, beckoning again. She added, feeling the pain again in her throat, "When I'm old—older than the old woman who taught me to make the hexes—come for me then.''

"I will."

"Promise me. That you will bring me black pearls and sing me into the sea when I am old.''

"I promise."

She lifted her hands to touch his shoulders, his face. But already his thoughts were turning from her, receding with the tide. Her hands dropped, empty but for the black pearl. He kissed her softly, left her to the empty air.

She stepped out of the tide's reach, and bumped into Lyo. He steadied her. The king rode his horse past the tide line, up to dry sand, and dismounted.

"I don't know if she'll come," he said to Lyo.

"How did you call her before?"

"I didn't . . . at least, not knowingly. We called each other, I think. I would walk along the tide line wanting her, and soon I would see her drifting behind the breakers, with her long, pale hair flowing behind her in the moonlight." His eyes went to his son yearning at the tide's edge. "If she can't hear me now, it seems that she should hear him. That his longing would reach out to her."

"Yes," Lyo said gently. One of the hexes in his hands caught light; white fire blazed between his fingers. It pulled at the king's eyes.

"What will you do with those?"

"I'm not sure yet. . . . I'll think of something."

"You are young to be so adept."

"I pay attention to things," Lyo said. "That's all." His attention strayed to the sea; they all watched it. Something must happen, Peri thought, entranced by the glittering, weaving, breaking path of the moonlight across the water to . . . what? Something must happen.

Lyo gazed down at the moonlit weave in his hands. "Not fire," he whispered. "Here it is light. Moons and moonlight." He lifted a hex suddenly, threw it. Moonlight illumined it as it fell between the spires; an enormous, brilliant wheel of light cast its reflection across the water. Then the hex fell to the water, but did not sink. It floated, still shedding its reflection across the dancing waves. The angle of light changed. Peri's lips parted. Someone had caught it. The reflection no longer slid with the moving sea; it flung itself between the spires, a great web clinging from stone to stone just above the water, hiding the moonlit path across the sea from the watchers on the shore.

Lyo grunted in surprise. The king said tautly, "Are you doing that?"

"No."

Kir had moved toward the web; tide swirled around his knees. He seemed to have left them already. If the sea would not accept him, Peri thought, he would still be changed; even on land, the tides would roar, beckoning, louder than any human voice in his head. She hugged herself, chilled, marveling. Something moved through the fiery web between the spires, drifted beyond the breakers. . . .

The king made a soft sound. Waves rolled toward them, curled into long silver coils and broke, shuddering against the sand. Water frothed around Kir, twisting his cloak; he pulled it off, tossed it like a shadow into the tide and moved deeper into the sea. A pale, wet head appeared and disappeared in the surf. A glint of pearl, of bright fish scale . . . Lyo tossed another hex.

This one hit the sand, made a shivering maze of light that the tide could not wash away. The figure in the surf moved toward it. Her shoulders appeared, and her long, heavy, tide-tossed hair. Her robe, carried for her by the currents, dragged down as she walked on land. The tide loosed her slowly.

The king moved to meet her. He stopped at the edge of the wide, burning web. A wave rolled over it; she stepped through the water, unerringly to the hex's bright center. Kir, still in the surf, had turned toward her. Lyo tossed him a hex; it grew under his next step as he turned back to wade out of the water to his mother. But instead of aiding him, the hex seemed to trap him, bind him, helpless and bewildered, in the heart of the maze. Lyo murmured something; Peri, one cold hand at her mouth, shook him with the other.

"Lyo!"

He muttered something else, exasperated, then quieted. "Shh," he said, both to himself and Peri. "Wait. The sea is working and unworking its own spellbindings."

The sea-woman's wet hair flowed to her feet; her shoulders were bowed under the weight of pearl. Her heavy-lidded, night-blue eyes seemed expressionless as she studied the king. Then she said something, and Peri heard Lyo's breath fall in relief.

"What did she say?"

"She said 'You've changed.' "

"It happens," the king said, "to humans."

She spoke again. Peri looked at Lyo, opening her mouth; he stooped suddenly and picked a shell out of the sand.

"Here."

"What should I—"

He tapped his ear patiently. "Listen."

She held it to her ear and heard the voice of the sea.

"Then," Kir's mother said, "I have been angry for a long time." Her voice was distant, dreamlike, passing from chamber to chamber within the shell.

"Yes."

"I did not realize how long it was until I felt my son's desire to come back to the sea. Is it long, by human time?"

"Yes," the king said softly. "Many years."

"Then many years ago, for many nights, I waited for you in the tide, and you did not come and you did not tell my why."

"You were like a dream to me. I had to turn away from you, return to my own world. I should have told you that."

"Yes."

"I should have told you that turning away from you was like turning away from wind and light. But I had to leave you. Can you forgive me?"

She lifted her hands slightly, opened them, as if letting something unseen fall. "I took your land-born child because I wanted you to have my child, our child. To love him as you could no longer love me. So you would look at him and remember me always."

"I did," he whispered.

"But I took your other son. I was angry, I made my anger into a chain, and changed your bright-haired son into something you would never see, never recognize. Can you forgive me for that?"

"How can I not, when I helped you forge that chain? All the twists and turns in it, your fault, my fault . . ."

"I kept him so long in that shape I nearly forgot what he was. Only the chain remembered my anger. Then one day the chain stretched beyond my magic and broke the surface of the sea. I could not hide your dragon-son any longer. He swam among the fishers, until their eyes turned to gold. And then even the gold vanished, my chain disappeared. . . ."

"So you let the sea-dragon take his shape on land?"

"No. I did nothing. The magic was out of my hands; it had become confused, unraveled. I had begun to hear my own son calling me, and I looked for him, but I could not reach him. All I could do was to disturb the fishers with small sea-spells, hoping they would go to you for help, and that you would find me." She sighed a little, a soft, distant breaking wave. "And you have finally come."

"To give you back our son. And to take mine out of the sea, bring him into the world where he belongs."

"I hope I have not kept him too long, that it is not too late for him in your world."

"I don't think so. But," he added, his voice low, weaving in and out of the sound of the breakers, "I have loved your restless sea-child, and taking him, you take another piece out of my heart. If there's a price to pay for his passage into the sea, that's all I have to give."

"There is no price." Her voice shook. "His desire is his path. But you must free him."

"I send him freely back. . . ." He paused, his eyes on her moonlit face, the pearls glowing here and there with a muted, silky light. "I was so young then, only a few years older than Kir, when I first saw you."

"I remember."

"It seems strange that, looking at your changeless face, I am not still that young man, walking beside the sea on a summer night, when all the stars seemed to have fallen into the water and you rose up out of the tide shaking stars out of your hair."

She smiled her delicate, careful smile; this time it had more warmth. "I remember. Your heart sang to the sea. I heard it, deep in my coral tower, and followed the singing. Humans say the sea sings to them and traps them, but sometimes it is the human song that traps the sea. Who knows where the land ends and the sea begins?"

"The land begins where time begins," the king said. "And it is time for Kir to leave me. Is it too late for him in your world?"

She turned her head, looked at Kir for the first time. Kir swayed a little, as if she or the undertow had pulled him off-balance. But still he could not step out of the web. She turned back to the king, her smile gone.

"I can hardly see his human shape, he is so much of the Undersea. His body is a shadow, his bones are fluid as water."

"Is it too late?"

"No. But he must leave your time now. No wonder he sang at me like the tide." Her shoulders were dragging wearily at the constant pull of the earth; even her hair seemed too heavy for her. "I must go now."

"Take him."

"I will. But you must free him." She lingered; waves covered the web under her feet, withdrew. It seemed to Peri that the king moved, or the sea-woman moved, or maybe the tide swirling about them made them only seem to move toward one another. For a moment, their faces looked peaceful. Then the woman said something too soft to carry past the web. She turned, stepped back into the sea, and melted into the foam.

Kir gave a cry of sorrow and despair that stopped Peri's heart. He turned, struggling against the web to follow the tide. But still he seemed trapped; he could only stand half in air, half in water, buffeted by waves that drenched him from head to foot but did not change him.

"Do something," Peri whispered. Tears slid down her face. "Lyo—"

"Do something," the king said, his voice sharp with anguish. "She said we must free him. Free him."

Lyo stared at the hexes in his hands. "They're so unpredictable," he murmured, baffled. "Peri, when you made them, did you say something over them? Or when you threw them into the sea?"

"I don't know, I don't know," she said distractedly. "I shouted at the sea—"

"What did you shout?"

"I don't know. Something—I was angry." Then she stopped. The world quieted around her, so hard was she thinking, suddenly. A lazy spring tide idled behind the spires . . . a malicious sea to be hexed. And like Kir's mother, she had woven her anger into a shape. . . . She felt the cold then, a chill of night, a chill of wonder. "I did it," she breathed. "Oh, Lyo, I did it."

"What did you do?" he and the king said together.

"I hexed the sea!" She drew wind into her lungs then, and shouted so hard it seemed there must be windows and doors slapping open all over the village, people putting their sleepy faces out. "I unhex you, Sea, I uncurse you! I take back everything I threw into you out of hate!'' She stopped, wiping tears off her face, then remembered the rest of her spellbinding. "May your spellbindings bind again, and your magic be unconfused. Open the door again between the land and the sea, and take this one last thing that I love, that belongs to land and sea, to us and you!''

The last of the hexes whirled across the water. They struck the great web hanging between the spires, the doorposts of the sea. Strands sagged, tore, revealing stars, half a moon, ragged pieces of moon-path. A wave hit Kir, knocked him off his feet. It curled around him, drew back. When they finally saw him again, he had surfaced and was sputtering in the deep waters beyond the surf.

He did not look back. He dove deeply, heading toward the spires; when he surfaced again, it was with a seal's movement, sleek, balanced, graceful. He dove, stayed underwater far too long, so long that those watching him had stopped breathing, too. Another strand of the web loosened, fell like an old rotting net unknotting as it dried. The white fierce light of it was fading as the web burned itself out, thread by thread, in the sea.

They saw Kir at last, dangerously near the spires. He should have been flung against the rocks, battered in the merciless swells. But he slid from wave to wave, an otter or a fish, nothing human. He watched the web above his head, strung between him and the wide, dark sea. When another thread dropped toward the water, he reached up, caught it. He dove then, dragging the white, gleaming strand down with him. The great hex unraveled wildly between the stones, then fell, burning, into the burning path of the moon.

They watched for a long time, but they did not see Kir again. Of all the crystal lights only the moon remained, still weaving its own web between the spires.

The king turned finally. They had all tried to follow Kir into the sea, it seemed; they were standing in the surf. Peri found Lyo's arm around her, holding her closely. She was numb with cold, too numb for sorrow, and felt that she would never be warm again. They stepped out of the tide. The king took Peri's face between his hands, kissed her forehead.

"Thank you." He looked at Lyo. "Thank you both." There was no great happiness in his voice, just a blank weariness that Peri understood. Kir was gone. Kir was . . . Then a movement in the surf startled her.

It was the sea-dragon, coming out. "He's walking," Peri whispered. "He's walking out of the sea."

He pulled a human body out of the swells, as patiently as he had dragged the sea-dragon's great body out. Once he stopped to catch something in his hand: a bit of froth, an edge of moonlight. He reached them finally, shivering, his gold brows knit.

"Kir is gone," he said. The king took off his damp cloak, pulled it around his wet son.

"Yes."

"I watched him. Now, I am gone."

"No," Peri said, as the king looked at him puzzledly, "you have left the sea. You are here."

"I am here." He looked at his father, his expression hesitant, complex. "Your eyes want to see Kir."

"Kir wished to leave. He needed to leave."

"You are the king who had two sons."

"Yes."

The sea-dragon's shoulders moved slightly, as if feeling, one last time, the weight of the chain. "The sea did not want me. If you do not want me, maybe Peri will."

Peri nodded; Lyo shook his head. The king smiled a little, touched the sea-dragon's face. "You look so like your mother. Her gentle eyes and her smile . . . That will help, when I explain where Kir has gone, and why you are suddenly in his place."

"And why I have no name in the world," the sea-dragon said simply. He stood silently, then, looking at the sea, the cold, uncomplicated world he would never see again.

"Will you miss the sea?" the king asked abruptly. "Will you stand at the tide's edge, like Kir, wanting to change your shape, to return to it?"

The sea-dragon met his eyes again. Something fully human surfaced in his face: a strength, a hint of pain, a loneliness no one would ever share. "I have left the sea," he said. He held out his hand, showed them the hex he had rescued from the tide. The strange light had burned down to ragged black threads. But a tiny crystal moon still hung in the center, glowing faintly with an inner light.

Lyo took it from him, touched the moon; it kindled a moment, luminous, fire-white. He lifted his eyes from it to gaze at Peri.

"Do you realize what you did?" he asked. "You managed to unbind, confuse, and otherwise snarl up the most powerful magic in the sea."

Her face burned. "I'm sorry. I never thought it would work."

"You're sorry? When you threw the hexes into the water and confused the sea's magic, you caused the chain to stretch beyond its bounds, break the surface between land and sea, so that the sea-dragon could finally take a look at the world.''

''But I trapped Kir on land, he couldn't get into the sea.''

''Peri,'' Lyo said patiently. ''You're not listening.''

''I am, too,'' she said.

''You're not paying attention.''

''Lyo, what are you—'' She stopped suddenly, blinking at him. ''I'm not paying attention,'' she whispered.

''You're swarming with magic like a beehive, Periwinkle.''

''I must be. . . . I'd better watch what I hex.''

''At the very least.'' His eyes narrowed slightly, glittering in the moonlight, fascinating her. ''Now tell me this. The night the sea-dragon dragged itself out of the sea for the first time, with you watching, did you happen to say anything to make it do that?''

''No,'' she said, surprised.

''Think, Peri.''

''Well, I was just watching the sky and the waves, thinking of Kir and wishing . . .''

''Wishing what?''

''Wishing that he could be . . .'' Her voice faltered; she stared at the magician, not seeing him but the dark, star-flecked sea. ''I said it. I said, 'I wish you were just a little more human.' But I meant Kir, not the sea-dragon!''

''So,'' the king murmured. ''The sea-dragon, passing by at the moment, came out of the sea, a little bit human every night.'' He was smiling, a smile like his sea-son's, never quite free. ''You have strange and wonderful gifts, Peri. You helped both my sons with your magic. Even more with your friendship." He sighed. "I wish you could have been powerful enough to keep Kir out of the sea, but in the world and under the sea, there is probably not enough magic for that. At least you brought this one out." He put a hand on the sea-dragon's shoulder; the sea-dragon started.

"You are touching me," he said wistfully. The king's face changed; he drew the sea-dragon into his arms.

"Yes," he said gruffly. "I am holding you. Humans touch. If they are foolish enough or wise enough. Come home with me now before you change your mind and follow the tide." He looked at Lyo. "I'll need your help with him. Can you stay?"

Lyo nodded, his mouth pulling upward into his private, slanting smile. "Oh, yes. I have some unfinished business involving periwinkles."

"Periwinkles," the sea-dragon echoed curiously.

"Small blue flowers," the magician said, and for the first time they heard both the king and the sea-dragon laugh.

Thirteen

The next few days, to Peri, seemed as colorless and dreary as the water she dumped out of her bucket at the day's end. The sky was a brilliant blue; the gorse, in full bloom, covered the cliffs with clouds of gold. The fishers went out every day; there were no more tales of singing sirens or ghostly ships. Peri, for the first time in weeks, could get a full night's sleep.

But she still woke late at night, listening for the sea-dragon; she still looked for Kir on the tide line; she still searched the sea between the spires, without thinking, watching for something unexpected, a message from the Undersea. She felt numb inside. All the magic was gone, nothing would ever happen to her again. Only the black pearl in her pocket told her that mystery had come into her life and gone, leaving her stranded at the tide's edge, yearning.

Mystery had stranded the villagers, too; they still longed, like Peri, for its return.

"I thought you said the mage was back," Enin said to Peri one afternoon, when she was putting her cleaning things away.

"He is," she said shortly.

"Then where is he?"

She shrugged, morose. "With the king, I guess."

Mare glanced at her oddly. "What's he doing there? We hired him."

"Helping with his son."

"What's the matter with Kir?"

"Nothing." She swallowed. "Nothing now. It's not Kir," she added, since everyone would know soon enough, anyway. "Kir went into the sea."

"He drowned?" Carey and Enin said incredulously.

"No." She took her apron off, bundled it up, hardly listening to what she was saying. "Kir went back to the sea. His mother is a sea-woman. The king's son by his true wife was the sea-dragon. That's why it was chained—the sea-woman was angry with the king. But she also loved him, which is why she gave him Kir. He came to my house at night in his human shape to learn words. The sea-dragon did. He's with the king now." They were staring at her, not moving, not speaking. She pulled her hair away from her eyes tiredly. "So that's where Lyo is, probably." She took the black pearl out of her pocket. "Kir gave me this before he left."

"Kir?" Carey's voice squeaked. The rest of her was immobile. Peri was silent, gazing at the pearl, remembering the full moon, Kir's hands in her hair, his promise to sing her into the sea. She lifted her head; faces blurred a moment, under tears she forced away.

"He used to come and talk to me. . . ." She slid the

146

pearl back into her pocket and pulled her cloak off a hook.

Carey whispered, "What's he like? The new prince?"

"He has gold hair and blue eyes. Like his mother had. He can't talk very well yet, but he learns fast." She put her cloak over her arm and went to the door.

Mare said fiercely, "Girl, you take one more step, I will throw a bucket at you. You come upstairs with us and tell the story properly from one end to the other. You can't just go and leave us here with a jumble like that: sea-women, secret sons, princes wandering into your house at night giving you black pearls. . . ."

"I don't understand," Carey said plaintively, staring at Peri, "why it all happened to her. Look at her!"

They did, until she fidgeted. "I washed my hair yesterday," she said defensively. Mare groaned. Enin grinned.

She drifted to her mother's house the next afternoon. The days were growing longer; the air was full of delicate, elusive scents. Evening lay in dusky, silken colors over the sea. The sea-kingdom seemed very near the surface, just beneath the lingering shades of sunset. Peri found her mother leaning over the gate, watching the distant sea. Behind her, the garden was sprouting tidy rows of green shoots; there was a peculiar absence of weeds.

Peri's mother smiled as Peri came up the street. She opened the gate; they both leaned over it then, watching. Peri's eyes slid to her mother's hands. There was black dirt on her fingers, even a streak on her face.

"You've been gardening!"

"I thought I'd pull a few thistles. It seemed a nice

day for it." Her voice sounded less weary than usual; the lines on her face had eased. Had the sea, Peri wondered suddenly, set her free, too?

They watched the fishing boats come into the harbor. When the last of them had slipped past the harbor-mouth, Peri's mother sighed, not in sadness, it seemed to Peri, but in relief that everyone was safely home. She said, "I miss you, Peri. The house seems empty suddenly. Do you think you might like to come back?"

Peri looked at her. The old woman's house felt that way, these days, too quiet, as empty as her heart. "Come back?"

"I never even asked where you've been living."

"Out at the old woman's house, near the stones. After she disappeared, I stayed there."

Her mother nodded. "I guessed, when I thought about it at all, that you might be there. I wonder where she got to, the old woman."

"Maybe," Peri said softly, "maybe into the sea. Maybe someone . . . someone special left a pearl on her doorstep and sang to her until she followed the singing."

"There is no land beneath the sea. You told me that."

"Well," Peri sighed, "I don't know everything, do I?"

"Do you think you'd like to come back?"

Peri turned to glance at the house. The door was open; a last thread of light pooled across the threshold. It might be nice, she thought, to have someone to talk to, now that her mother was talking again.

"Maybe," she said. "For a little while."

"You need some new clothes, child."

"I know. I forget things like that."

"You're growing again."

"I know." She picked at a splinter in the gate, her eyes straying to the sea. The last light faded; a thin band of blue stretched across the horizon, the shadow of night. She sighed. What did it matter where she lived? "All right," she said. "I'm tired of my cooking, anyway." She swallowed a sudden burning; her face ducked behind her hair. "What does it matter?" she whispered. She felt her mother's arm across her shoulders. The sea began to darken, the night-shadow widened, a deep, deep blue, the darkest shades of mother-of-pearl. . . .

They heard a whistling through the dusk. Peri jumped, for it had shifted abruptly from the street to her elbow.

"Lyo!"

"Goodness," her mother said, startled. Lyo gave her a deep bow, standing in her weed pile.

"This is Lyo," Peri explained. "He is the magician who turned the gold chain into flowers."

"What gold chain?" her mother said bemusedly. "What flowers?"

"Where did you get those clothes?" Peri asked. Lyo had put aside his scuffed and gorse-speckled leather and wool for a more familiar mage's robe of wheat and gold. It made him look taller somehow; even his hair had settled down.

"The king gave it to me. He said I was beginning to smell a bit briny."

"Oh. It looks very—very—"

He nodded imperturbably. "Thank you. It'll do for now. It'd be hard to row a boat in, though."

"Are you?"

"Am I what?"

"Going to sea to get the gold? The fishers keep asking me that."

"Oh," he said, chuckling.

"Well, are you?"

"Not exactly."

She looked at him, baffled. His eyes shifted colors mysteriously: the green of the seedlings, the brown of the earth; they pulled at her attention until she blinked herself free. "How is the sea-dragon?" she asked, since he wouldn't tell her about the gold.

"Aidon," Lyo said. "The king named him that."

"Is he learning to talk any better?"

"He's doing very well. I'm teaching him to read. Yesterday we added and subtracted periwinkles. That's what I—"

"A talking sea-dragon named Aidon," Peri's mother interrupted. "What are you talking about? A sea-dragon reading books?"

Lyo's brows rose. "You didn't tell her?"

"No."

"Tell me what? What sea-dragon? What gold chain?" She watched her daughter and the strange-eyed magician look at one another uncertainly. "Peri, what have you been doing while I haven't been paying attention?"

"Oh." She took a long breath. "It's a little hard to explain."

"Then you'd both better come in and have some supper and explain it to me," her mother said, sounding so much like her old self that Peri felt a sudden bubble of laughter inside her.

Lyo sat at the hearth, beginning in a calm and methodical fashion to explain while her mother chopped up carrots and onions for soup. Peri kept interrupting him; he gave up finally and let her tell the story for a while. Peri's mother sat down slowly in the middle of it, a paring knife in one hand and an onion in the other. The color came back into her face as she listened. She laughed and cried at different parts of the tale, and then, as Peri told her about the king and the sea-woman meeting each other under the moon, a stillness settled into her face, like the calm over water after a storm. She had finished her sea-journey, Peri realized; she had gone and come back to the familiar world, the one where she sang old sea chanteys and knew the names of all the shells on the beach.

She was silent for a long time when Lyo and Peri finished the story. Peri knew what she was seeing: the long, brilliant, fleeting path of sunlight between the spires. She saw the onion in her hand and got up finally. "Well," she said softly. "Well."

"That's partly why I came here," Lyo said. "The sea-dragon misses Peri."

"I can guess why. She's the first girl he ever saw."

"Yes." Lyo stopped a moment, his expression awry. "Yes. So the king wondered if Peri might consider coming to the summer house to teach Aidon again."

"You mean after work?" Peri asked, dazed.

"Peri, you can forget the brushes, the buckets. The king will pay you well for teaching. And the sea—Aidon will be happy to see you again. He likes being human, but he misses you. He had to give up his brother; he shouldn't have to lose you, too. Would you like to do that?"

"Teach the sea-dragon in the king's house?" She nodded vigorously, thinking of the prince's blue-eyed smile, his need of her. "Oh, yes. But doesn't the king want you to stay? I don't know very much beyond adding and subtracting."

"Oh, I'll stay awhile. Teach you a little magic," he added nonchalantly. "If you like. Just so you won't get into trouble. . . ." He paused again, staring so hard at a wooden nail in the floorboards that she thought it might rise out of the floor. Then he shook himself, ruffled his hair with both hands, and met her eyes. "Are you?" he inquired.

"What?"

"Planning to fall in love with any more princes?"

She thought about it, gazing back at him. Then she sighed deeply, her hand sliding into her pocket to touch the black pearl that held all her memories. "I don't think so. One prince is enough in one lifetime."

"Good," Lyo said with relief. He pulled beer out of the air then, and yellow daffodils, and a loaf of hot bread that looked as if it had come straight out of the innkeeper's kitchen.

"Lyo!" Her mother, face in the flowers, was laughing.

"It's all right, he'll get his payment tomorrow." He poured a basket of early strawberries into Peri's lap. "There will be a sea harvest of periwinkles coming in on the morning tide that this village will never forget."

Peri, her mouth falling open, saw periwinkles turning to gold all down the beach as the sea swept them tidily out of itself. "That will make Carey happy."

"Perhaps," Lyo said. "Perhaps not even that will make Carey happy. It's an odd thing, happiness. Some people take happiness from gold. Or black pearls. And some of us, far more fortunate, take their happiness from periwinkles." He leaned over Peri, impelled by some mysterious impulse, kissed her gently. "I've been wanting to do that for some time," he told her. "But you always had one king's son or another at hand."

Like him, she was flushed under her untidy hair. "Well," she said, "now I don't."

"Now you don't." He watched her, smiling but uncertain. Then, still uncertain, he sat down beside her mother to help her clean shrimp. Peri's eyes strayed to the window. But the magician's lean, nut-brown face, constantly hovering between magic and laughter, came between her and the darkening sea. After a while, watching him instead, she began to smile.

About the Author

PATRICIA A. MCKILLIP discovered the joys of writing when she was fourteen, endured her teen-age years in the secret life of her stories, plays, and novels, and has been writing ever since—except for a brief detour when she thought she would be a concert pianist.

She was born in Salem, Oregon, and has lived in Arizona, California, and the England that is the setting for *The House on Parchment Street*. After a number of years in San Jose, where she received an MA in English from San Jose State University, she moved to San Francisco, where she now lives.

Miss McKillip has also written *The Throme of the Erril of Sherill*, *The Forgotten Beasts of Eld*, *The Night Gift*, and *The Quest of the Riddle-Master*, a fantasy trilogy.